The Case of the Two Pearl Necklaces

By A. E. Fielding

Originally published in 1936

The Case of the Two Pearl Necklaces

Published by Intrepid Ink, LLC

Intrepid Ink, LLC provides full publishing services to authors of fiction and non-fiction books, eBooks and websites. From editing to formatting, to publishing, to marketing, Intrepid Ink gets your creative works into the hands of the people who want to read them.
Find out more at www.IntrepidInk.com.

ISBN 13: 978-1-937022-69-3

Printed in the United States of America

RESURRECTED PRESS CLASSIC MYSTERY CATALOGUE

Journeys into Mystery
Travel and Mystery in a More Elegant Time

The Edwardian Detectives
Literary Sleuths of the Edwardian Era

Gems of Mystery
Lost Jewels from a More Elegant Age

Anne Austin
One Drop of Blood
The Black Pigeon
Murder at Bridge

E. C. Bentley
Trent's Last Case: The Woman in Black

Ernest Bramah
Max Carrados Resurrected:
The Detective Stories of Max Carrados

Agatha Christie
The Secret Adversary
The Mysterious Affair at Styles

Octavus Roy Cohen
Midnight

Freeman Wills Croft
The Ponson Case
The Pit Prop Syndicate

J. S. Fletcher

The Herapath Property
The Rayner-Slade Amalgamation
The Chestermarke Instinct
The Paradise Mystery
Dead Men's Money
The Middle of Things
Ravensdene Court
Scarhaven Keep
The Orange-Yellow Diamond
The Middle Temple Murder
The Tallyrand Maxim
The Borough Treasurer
In the Mayor's Parlour
The Saftey Pin

R. Austin Freeman

The Mystery of 31 New Inn from the Dr. Thorndyke Series
John Thorndyke's Cases from the Dr. Thorndyke Series
The Red Thumb Mark from The Dr. Thorndyke Series
The Eye of Osiris from The Dr. Thorndyke Series
A Silent Witness from the Dr. John Thorndyke Series
The Cat's Eye from the Dr. John Thorndyke Series
Helen Vardon's Confession: A Dr. John Thorndyke Story
As a Thief in the Night: A Dr. John Thorndyke Story
Mr. Pottermack's Oversight: A Dr. John Thorndyke Story
Dr. Thorndyke Intervenes: A Dr. John Thorndyke Story
The Singing Bone: The Adventures of Dr. Thorndyke
The Stoneware Monkey: A Dr. John Thorndyke Story
The Great Portrait Mystery, and Other Stories: A Collection of Dr. John Thorndyke and Other Stories
The Penrose Mystery: A Dr. John Thorndyke Story
The Uttermost Farthing: A Savant's Vendetta

The Bride of a Moment
Faulkner's Folly
The Diamond Pin
The Gold Bag
The Mystery of the Sycamore
The Come Back

Raoul Whitfield
Death in a Bowl

And much more!
Visit ResurrectedPress.com
for our complete catalogue

FOREWORD

About the Author

The identity of the author is as much a mystery as the plots of the novels. Two dozen novels were published from 1924 to 1944 as by Archibald Fielding, A. E. Fielding, or Archibald E. Fielding, yet the only clue as to the real author is a comment by the American publishers, H.C. Kinsey Co. that A. E. Fielding was in reality a "middle-aged English woman by the name of Dorothy Feilding whose peacetime address is Sheffield Terrace, Kensington, London, and who enjoys gardening." Research on the part of John Herrington has uncovered a person by that name living at 2 Sheffield Terrace from 1932-1936. She appears to have moved to Islington in 1937 after which she disappears. To complicate things, some have attributed the authorship to Lady Dorothy Mary Evelyn Moore nee Feilding (1889-1935), however, a grandson of Lady Dorothy denied any family knowledge of such authorship. The archivist at Collins, the British publisher, reports that any records of A. Fielding were presumably lost during WWII. Birthdates have been given variously as 1884, 1889, and 1900. Unless new information comes to light, it would appear that the real authorship must remain a mystery.

Greg Fowlkes
Editor-In-Chief
Resurrected Press
www.ResurrectedPress.com

CHAPTER ONE: A WEDDING IS ANNOUNCED

Arthur Walsh hurried up the steps of Friars Halt, across the big hall and along a passage to his father's study. The footman looked after him in surprise. He had never seen Mr. Arthur in a hurry before. Then he saw him pause before a bowl of flowers as though enchanted by their beauty; and neither had he ever seen him do that before. Arthur stood so long staring at the delphinium spires that the footman had perforce to leave him entranced. But Arthur was not spellbound. Once he cast a glance at the study door that suggested an inexperienced lion tamer about to enter the cage of his fiercest animal, and by no means liking the prospect.

He was twenty-eight years old, fairly tall, and had a face that began well in a good forehead, but ended in a weak chin. Finally, after one more prolonged stare at the flowers, he opened the door beside him and went on in. Colonel Walsh sat looking into the fire, an open letter in his hand. He had a long thin face with a tightly compressed mouth and steadfast grey eyes. Taken together, eyes and mouth gave him a curiously daunting air. Not to Colonel Walsh did people turn to ask the way. Not of him would children inquire the time. He had never to suffer from the club bore. One glance from him, and straggler, child or bore passed on.

"Gerald is dead," Colonel Walsh said, turning to face his son. His voice was deep and powerful.

For a second Arthur looked as though he could not place his brother Gerald. "When did it happen?" he asked after a second. "Poor old Gerald! Where was it?"

"In Smyrna. Circus performance. The roof crashed in, and Gerald was among the dead. His passport gave his name, and Raeburn—who's consul there—identified the body."

Colonel Walsh spoke abruptly. Looking into Arthur's face, it came to him with a sudden and quite unexpected wrench that Gerald, the brilliant though unreliable, was dead, and that Arthur, the dull one, alone remained to him. For he had but the two sons.

"It seems only yesterday that he walked through that door laughing and swinging his cap," Arthur said, drawing a deep breath.

A spasm crossed his father's face.

"He lied to me," he said evenly, but with a suggestion in his low tone of answering some accusation. "Lied! He knew that is the one thing I won't stand, yet he did it. You owned up. He lied!" He drew a difficult breath as he added: "Gerald was given to lying."

Arthur nodded. Gerald was. As a rule he had done it well, but on the occasion in question his father had had inside knowledge, and so Gerald had been turned adrift with his clothes and a hundred pounds in money. That had been nearly three years ago. And now Gerald was dead . . .! Arthur looked almost curiously at his father. The Colonel had clearly had a painful shock. One wouldn't have thought he would have cared!

"I came in to tell you something, Pater," Arthur said abruptly. "I'm afraid it's rather an inopportune moment. . . ."

Colonel Walsh straightened up, looking inquiringly at him, his formidable, narrow face as hawk-like as usual. "Well?"

His son looked at him with something harder in his eye than one might have expected.

"I'm going to be married."

"And who is the lady?" Colonel Walsh leant forward sharply. One would say that he guessed the name, or believed that he did.

"You've never met her, I think. Her name is Violet Finch."

His father's face became blank. Colonel Walsh had felt certain that now that Ann Lovelace was back in England, and unmarried, Arthur would try his luck once again— and this time with success. He had assumed that this would be the announcement. But a Violet Finch . . .?

"And her people arc?" inquired Colonel Walsh.

"Nothing much," Arthur gave a little deprecatory smile. "Her father was a barrister. He's dead. Her mother—"He hesitated.

"She's not the Mrs. Finch surely?" the Colonel interposed.

"I really can't possibly say whom you mean by that," was the acid retort. "Violet's mother is a lady who, left quite penniless, started some night-clubs which for a time succeeded very well. And therefore made her a lot of money—and enemies."

Colonel Walsh was grimly silent. So it was the Mrs. Finch! His mouth was tighter lipped than usual. So tight that at a glance it looked as though he had only one hp.

"You'll like Violet, Pater. She's as straight as —as you are yourself. Outspoken—forthright—not at all a woman of the world; but she has a vitality that I envy!" Arthur hurried on.

"That's to the good," the Colonel commented. "Well, Arthur, I won't pretend that I would not have been pleased if it had been some one your aunt and I know, whose people we know; but any one you love will receive the welcome due to my son's wife. When is the wedding to be?"

"Next month. I don't want a long engagement, and Violet isn't very happy at home. She's not in the least a cabaret girl, sir. You don't need to be afraid of that."

"How did you come to meet her? " Colonel Walsh asked.

"At one of the Little Owls." Those were Mrs. Finch's famous night-clubs. "She looked such a country girl, such a fish out of water, that I wondered to see her there. . . . I don't say I wasn't a bit taken aback when I found out who she was —I didn't catch her name when we were introduced —but by that time I had talked to her and— well, you can't explain these things, can you?" he added with a deprecating laugh.

Colonel Walsh agreed that you couldn't, then went into the question of the increased income his son could expect at his marriage. Colonel Walsh was a very wealthy man indeed. Principally interested in tobacco, his range included many other things as well. At the present moment Arthur was in his father's head office and earned, or rather was paid, a salary of five thousand a year. In addition to this he had his allowance of one thousand. Quite a comfortable total, even in these days. He had been in the Army, and at that time his father had considered a thousand quite sufficient for his needs. Arthur had thought otherwise, and there had finally come a night when the Colonel faced him with a pile of bills before him and Arthur next morning had sent in his papers. It was after that that he had entered his father's office—and Gerald had gone abroad.

"I started some years ago," the Colonel went on, "a sort of marriage fund for each of you two boys. Then when Gerald failed me, and dropped out of the reckoning, the two funds were made into one. It stands at fifty thousand now, and you shall have my cheque for it as my wedding present."

"You're more than generous, Pater," Arthur said gratefully.

Colonel Walsh made a gesture. "I appreciate the way you've kept nothing back about your future wife. If only Gerald had realised that I'll overlook anything but deception, he would probably be here alive to-day—not killed in an Asia Minor circus."

Arthur nodded. He said nothing. Gerald had been "Gerald." Handsome, debonair, careless of money, and of whether what he said tallied with facts or not. The end had been inevitable, as he had often warned Gerald that it must be.

When he was alone, the Colonel sat on, his sad thoughts with Gerald rather than with Arthur. His sister, Lady Monkhouse, found him still there, staring into the fire, his pipe practically out. She had not yet learnt Arthur's news. Arthur had always been her favourite, but she heard of his engagement with almost comic fury.

"Arthur! Arthur! to be caught by the daughter of that dreadful woman!" She was inconsolable. "Oh, I saw her once; great big, bouncing, noisy bold-eyed creature! If only Ann Lovelace had taken him, when he was head over ears in love with her."

"In those days there was Gerald," Colonel Walsh said in a level voice. "Arthur was the younger son—then."

Lady Monkhouse was shocked. Truths often had that effect on her.

"Ann would have been a wonderful wife for Arthur," she went on, "and he adored her. . . ."

"At that time," finished the Colonel dryly. "Pity he couldn't have taken a fancy to Kitty."

Lady Monkhouse raised her nicely plucked eyebrows. Kitty was the Colonel's niece, and lived with them.

"Kitty," Lady Monkhouse said now. "Well, hardly! I think, George, that Arthur is far too clever to be content with little Kitty! Now Ann would be his intellectual equal, and socially, of course—with her connections— she's the Duchess's favourite niece—anything would have been possible. . . . But this Finch girl . . .! I can't believe it! I simply cannot!"

Arthur came in. "Talking about Violet?" he asked gaily.

His aunt looked sombrely back at him. "Don't expect me to congratulate you," she said bitterly. "It would be a mockery!"

Upon which there was a very fine family quarrel. Arthur, usually very cautious in his words, raved about his aunt's prejudices and Violet Finch's excellences, and his father took his part. So did Kitty when she came in, lured, it must be confessed, by curiosity at the loud tones of the talk. Kitty was a palefaced slip of a girl with big, brown eyes and an air of youth and freshness and candour that far outweighed mere prettiness in Colonel Walsh's opinion. He would have considered Arthur a very lucky man indeed to have won Kitty. And he had thought that Kitty's heart was turning a little to Arthur. Now he hoped that he had been mistaken. He would not like to think her young life hurt beneath his roof. . . .

Arthur finally stalked away in a fine temper, leaving his aunt looking rather ill-at-ease. She had spoken very hastily . . . she had said some things anent Violet Finch. and the family of Finch that might well have been put differently; and some that were best not put at all.

"I had no idea you knew so much about night-clubs," her brother remarked dryly.

Colonel Walsh had the masculine idea that family plain speaking was his own prerogative, that as long as he did not swear at things no one else should do so. He never could understand why a king of Israel needed to get a prophet to curse the people for him. . . . That always seemed to him one of the few things a man should do for himself, if done at all.

"Oh, I've been to the Little Owls. A couple of years back every one went. That Finch woman made a sinful amount of money out of it. Simply incredible profits! Thousands there every night. . . . They gambled for enormous stakes upstairs in her private flat, it was whispered. Now I hear that the place is running down as speedily as it shot up. And to think that Arthur—of all young men! I thought he, at least, was sensible!"

Walsh winced. She was referring obliquely to Gerald, and somehow—just now—it hurt.

"Look here, Kitty," Lady Monkhouse wound up. "You're going to town for a week—to get your brother's flat ready for his return. Do call on these Finches and give us your opinion of the girl. I may be prejudiced, though I'm sure I'm not. . . ."

Kitty raised no objection to this informal scrutiny of the future Mrs. Arthur Walsh, agreeing to do so within the next few days.

Chapter Two: Violet Finch Wears Some Fine Pearls at a Dance

Three weeks later Mrs. Finch was giving a dance, and apparently at the same time giving the lie to current rumours of her being absolutely on the rocks. True, it was to celebrate her daughter's engagement to Arthur Walsh, that wealthy catch, but, even so, it was very lavish.

There was dancing in two splendid ballrooms, there was bridge in half a dozen card-rooms, and there would be supper such as only the Merveille Hotel could supply in its spacious supper-room. And there was also a Sicilian Marionette show which had caught her guests' fancy.

Kitty Walsh had just been watching the marionettes. At first with keen amusement; but suddenly they had become not funny at all—instead, a sort of ghastly parody on life. They looked so incredibly alive, their actions seemed too intelligent, and yet they were only puppets that were dancing, and making love, and even committing murders with such energy and dash. She shot a glance at Ronald Mills beside her; it had been his idea that in lieu of another dance they should watch the Show for a while. He caught her eye and followed her back into the ballroom.

"What do you think of them, Miss Walsh? Good, eh?"

Ronald Mills always spoke in a loud voice as though any one, near or far, must be interested in bis opinions, his questions, his lightest utterance. He was a long, thin man with a long, thin face, long, thin hps, long, thin teeth, and a very cynical smile. Well turned out, he always slouched, whether walking or sitting, and whenever possible had a cigarette dangling from his lip.

In age he looked around thirty, but an extremely ripe thirty. His voice was unexpectedly big and booming.

She did not reply. What did she think of them?

"You seen them, Walsh?" Mills called to her cousin, as the latter passed them with his fiancee.

They stopped at the question and came towards Kitty. Arthur's blue eyes were twinkling like a mischievous schoolboy's below the sandy eyebrows that seemed to begin indefinitely nowhere and end vaguely nowhere— like his chin.

"Yes, funny show. Clever, and all that. . . ."

"Did you like them?" Mills asked carelessly.

"I dunno. What did you think of them, Vi?"

"Lousy," came the instant answer, as Miss Finch surveyed herself complacently over Arthur's shoulder in a wall-mirror. Afterwards, Kitty thought that the two ropes of pearls around Violet's throat should have been rubies, like drops of blood, so singular and so sinister a part did they play in the tragedy that followed. Violet Finch was handsome, in a heavy way. She had a masterful eye, but she was looking her flamboyant best to-night.

"I didn't care much for them, either," echoed Arthur. And Mills laughed.

Mrs. Finch came up. She had married a man called Gray, a year ago, but she remained Mrs. Finch to every one but the registrar. She was a little woman with deep-set eyes that were far too bright and unwinking. She was very plain, and used no make-up. Her dress was expensive enough, but carelessly put on. Her hands were restless, always fingering things on herself or on anything near her. She looked as though possessed of boundless determination and driving power.

"I thought them positively frightening," she said, joining in the talk, "actually sinister. I shouldn't like to be jerked about by a string, would you, Artie?" She laughed at her own words, and Mrs. Finch-Gray was more than plain, she was an ugly woman when she laughed. Her sharp chin poked forward, her mouth looked loose and frog-like.

Kitty was claimed for the dance and moved away.

Arthur shook his head vaguely. "Depends," he said cautiously.

"On what Vi thinks?" Mills asked with studied carelessness.

Mrs. Finch—as people continued to call her—gave him a sharply warning look that suggested anger. Mills was her business partner.

"Naturally, any man's guided by what his fiancee thinks," she said smoothly.

"Guided like the marionettes?" Mills flashed back at her with a suggestion of snapping his fingers at her vexation, as he strode forward to a woman in purple and silver and eagerly asked her to let him take her in to supper. This was Mrs. Yerkes, and Mills hoped very much to marry Mrs. Yerkes.

Arthur wrinkled his forehead and looked after him, then at Mrs. Finch.

"You two always sound to me as though you were sparring," he murmured. "Well, Vi, I must let that tiresome Lady Brygitte trample about on my toes for another round of the room." He moved away. But Violet, too, stood looking after Mills.

"He's a bit too clever," she said darkly.

"—And so sharp that he'll cut himself one of these days," finished her mother. For the moment the two were alone in a corner.

"You've got Arthur well broken in," Mrs. Finch murmured in a tone of grudging praise—as to a pupil.

Violet tossed her head.

"And we don't need your cracking the whip all the time, either!" she said ungratefully. "You and your marionettes! If it had been any one but Arthur he might have turned nasty!"

"And that's the thanks I get, is it?" Mrs. Finch demanded in a fierce whisper, as she thrust her face almost into her daughter's.

"I suppose you think you could have brought it off by yourself! It would be just like your conceit! No, no, my fine lady! It's your mother who's put you where you are, and don't you forget it!"

"You don't!" came from Violet, "and a nice fat sum of money you managed to borrow on the strength of my engagement to a rich man. Don't you suppose I know that?"

"And why not?" whispered her mother again. Then she fell silent, a tired look coming over her face. "And not a penny of it that I can stick to —yet," she went on. "These damned debts! They're enough to break down a horse. Debts everywhere, and you spending money like water. Who's to pay for that new car of yours?"

"Oh, I dunno," Violet said indifferently. "What about your new Daimler?"

"I only 'bought' that for this dance!" Mrs. Finch spoke meaningly and both women laughed outright. "I don't want dear Artie to smell a rat, and know just how deeply in the soup we really are, or would be, but for my having handled him just the way I did. The Daimler will be taken back to-morrow. It's all arranged. But I want a private word with you, Vi." Taking a key from her jewelled bag, she led her daughter into an empty card-room which she unlocked, and closed the door, standing against it.

"That sapphire pendant business was silly," she said then. "Luckily I made you find it before things got serious." Her words were light, but her eyes glittered. "By God!" She spoke with a sudden outflaming of fury. "If you think I've climbed up almost into safety to let you wreck me on its threshold, you don't know me even yet, my girl!" Her face was a daunting revelation of what she might be capable. Violet Finch stared at it in real fear. Then the face changed. Her mother hung up the curtains again, as it were, and spoke smoothly. "That aunt of his would be only too glad to ferret out anything against you."

"She can't!" Violet said, chin in air.

"No, I've seen to that," her mother retorted. "But you would have made a fool of yourself over Ronald Mills, if I hadn't stopped you."

"That's past," Violet said sullenly, picking up a paper from the table beside her.

"To go back, now, to the pendant," Mrs. Finch continued. "If I ever catch you trying games of that kind again before you're safely married to Arthur, you'll be sorry for yourself!" Again that look of latent ferocity swept up for a second, glowed like a red danger signal, and then dropped out of sight.

"Oh, all right!" Violet said sullenly. And then in a tone of intense surprise: "But what's my name doing here, on this paper?"

Mrs. Finch would have snatched it from her, but in physical strength Violet was her mother's superior.

"Why, it's something to do with my death!" She stared blankly at the paper in her hands.

"Oh, that!" Mrs. Finch said casually. "You knew, months ago, that I was going to sell the Reversion to the thousand your father left you a life interest in, which I bought from you last year. Well, I'm selling it to Gray." She and Violet always referred to her present husband by his surname. "For I must scrape every possible farthing together just now. What are you fussing about?"

"I'm not fussing—I'm asking." Violet laid the paper down again as she spoke. "What a funny thing to be doing to-night!"

"My affairs come up for hearing in the Bankruptcy Court to-morrow," her mother replied with really amazing indifference. "And I want to get rid of all I can to Gray first." She did not add that that was precisely why she had married again. Violet knew as much. So did Henry Gray.

"Well, it's not likely to do Gray much good," Violet laughed. After all, she was too well satisfied to-night to be vexed for long. "I feel as though I should live for another century." And before going back to the ballroom she paused to adjust the pearls afresh.

"They're to be mine," her mother said with a covetous look at their lustre.

"No, they're to be heirlooms, Arthur says. That's why he doesn't give them outright to me," Violet grumbled.

"I'll have a talk with him about them. 'Heirlooms,' indeed!" Mrs. Finch snorted.

"You'll find out that there's a stone wall in Arthur that you can't always climb over, mother. Even I can't," warned Violet as she opened the door again and returned to the dancing.

Over and over she fingered the superb pearls around her throat. She lifted her dark head still more proudly, and she had an arrogant carriage at all times. There were plenty of young women in the room, many of them prettier, most of them better born. But it was she, Violet Finch, who had captured the rich prize, Arthur Walsh.

Take Ann Lovelace, for instance, floating by at that minute in one of the newest dances. She made you feel as though your smartest clothes came from Woolworth's, yet she hadn't been able to get Arthur away, though she had tried hard enough.

Ann raised her eyes as she was passing, and paused a moment. They were light grey eyes, very clear and tranquil.

"How well you're looking to-night, Violet," she said kindly. "Of course, those exquisite pearls are a joy in themselves, but it isn't only the pearls, is it?" she murmured with a smile of comprehension.

Ann had a heart-shaped face, beautifully featured, and framed in light golden hair. She was a niece of the Duchess of Axminster—a favourite niece, it was said. She looked the part. Slender, witty, always charmingly dressed—she had an air of fragile grace, every glimpse of which Violet detested because it made her feel like a farmer's daughter in comparison. And she had an uneasy doubt as to what lay behind that appearance of friendliness which Ann had shown her since their meeting at Friars Halt a fortnight before.

Kitty Walsh could have told her, but Kitty was no mischief maker. She was, indeed, one of the very few people in the room that evening who thought that her cousin was not making a bad match. For Kitty rather liked Violet, though the liking did not extend to Violet's mother—nor to Ronald Mills, the young man who helped Mrs. Finch run the night-clubs that had once been so incredibly profitable to her.

"Cleaned everybody out?" Kitty asked her uncle as he suddenly appeared beside her.

Colonel Walsh was known to be a formidable bridge player. He smiled a little. Kitty could always get that tribute from him. "What are you staying on here for?" he asked genially. "You look as though you belonged in the schoolroom, you know." And he tweaked an end of the ribbon she wore round her long, full silk gown.

"Ah, my looks are deceptive—like Ann's!" she said lightly, and then coloured with vexation. The last words had slipped out.

"How you do dislike Ann!" her uncle teased, But his eyes were a little wistful as he glanced across at Ann's lovely figure in its dress of silver and jade.

"I do," Kitty said frankly. "She never gives herself away; and I hate people who never give themselves away!" She made a little face at him as she changed the subject. "I suppose there's no chance of Aunt Caroline altering her mind and turning up?" she queried as she caught sight of her aunt's intimate friend coming towards them.

Colonel Walsh shook his head. His sister had refused to come. The Colonel regretted the engagement, too. But he was no tyrant, though he had cut his eldest son off with a shilling—or, to be strictly accurate, with a hundred pounds.

"Your aunt fears that Arthur's making a sad mistake. So does Ambrose. So do I. But Arthur's been frank and straightforward about the whole thing, so I don't intend to interfere."

Colonel Walsh and Kitty were close confidantes.

"What's the mother like?" he asked now, glancing that way. "Looks like a respectable elderly governess. But what's she really like?"

"I detested her when I spent those three days with her, you know—when the flat had to have a new system of lighting put in."

The Colonel nodded.

"Do you mean she was offensive?" He bristled.

"Oh, dear, no! On the contrary. She was awfully pleasant to me. But I don't think I've ever disliked any one quite so much without any reason."

"Except Ann!" he chaffed back.

"Ann!" she said under her breath. "Violet Finch mayn't be all you would like Arthur's wife to be," she continued softly, "but she's ever so much better than Ann Lovelace. Ann's selfish. She has a horrid temper. You remember that we were at Bedington together, she and I. Oh, yes, she was 'Head Girl' in her last year. But none the less there were plenty of others who felt just as I did. Ann always intended to be ' Head Girl,' and so, of course, she pulled it off."

"I think your aunt hopes she will still draw Arthur away from Violet Finch."

"Not a chance!" Kitty said at once. "Arthur adores Violet. Absolutely!" There was a something in her young voice that made her uncle look away. It sounded like very far-off, very repressed pain.

"Anyway, those pearls that Ann helped her choose look superb ones," the Colonel said hurriedly. "On loan to-night, I take it, as they're to be his wedding present?"

"Yes, they're lent to her till then. She asked Ann to help her choose them." Kitty did not add that the two strings of pearls in question had been a staggering extravagance, even for so rich a lover as was Arthur Walsh.

Lady Norton came up to them just then. She was the close friend of her aunt whom Kitty had noticed a few moments before.

The Colonel soon went back to the card tables and Lady Norton drew Kitty down into a chair beside her. "I must say the cocktails are worth coming for," she said with a grin, "as one would expect! But who is the handsome man hovering around Mrs. Finch?"

"That's Ronald Mills. He's a sort of manager of hers. Looks after her night-clubs for her and so on . . ."

The other grunted and patted some fresh rouge on her cheek. "Funny relations you're going to have, my child!" she said frankly.

Kitty moved restlessly in her chair. "I think that's ungenerous!" she said warmly. "Arthur isn't marrying to please us. Why should he? He's most tremendously in love. And why not? Violet has all sorts of sterling qualities. She'll make him a splendid wife. He's been inclined to drift, you know, to take life easy. . . . Violet's a good fighter. She'll make him do his bit. And that's what Arthur needs."

"You mean to tell me you like the girl?" Lady Norton demanded incredulously. "Your aunt considers her impossible."

"But she's not impossible," Kitty said firmly. "She is not, really! She's very outspoken—and forthright. Uncle will love that in her. She's unselfish, too. She took no end of trouble when I lost my sapphire pendant while I stayed over a week-end with them. And it was Violet who finally unearthed it, caught fast in a curtain fringe, just before I left."

"And do you also like her mother?" demanded Lady Norton sarcastically.

Kitty was silent.

"I wonder what Ann's mother, Lady Rosemary, would say about her," Lady Norton went on meditatively—and meaningly. "She was, you know, the cause of Ann's step-brother shooting himself. Those night-clubs of hers were sinks of iniquity. I wanted to go to one, out of curiosity. But we were stationed at Malta while they were the rage. And now, of course, they've gone out completely. I hear that Mrs. Finch won't have a bean left when they're finally wound up." Lady Norton added with relish.

Kitty fidgeted silently. She did not care to be connected even distantly with Mrs. Finch. And, as another partner came up to release her, she took good care to keep away from her aunt's friends for the rest of the evening.

Chapter Three: Pearls Can Be At Once Very Useful And Very Dangerous

On the following evening Violet was playing bridge at Colonel Walsh's house in Grosvenor Square. He was presenting the house to Arthur as a wedding gift, together with a separate fund for its maintenance. Violet was very much to the fore on this occasion. A trifle self-assertive, and more than a trifle dictatorial.

But Arthur looked delighted to be allowed to breathe the same air as his divinity. He played badly. Violet, as always, played extremely well, and won quite a nice little sum from Ann Lovelace and her partner.

Ann handed over a couple of notes with a smile. "Nothing can resist you to-night, Violet. You ought to be at Grayham's," she said a little later, when Violet happened to be alone with her, making up in the cloakroom. Ann stretched out a lovely hand and laid a caressing finger-tip for a second on one of the pearls as they swung towards her at some movement of their wearer's.

"Where's that?" Violet asked.

"He's a man from South Africa. He has a flat close by, and lets a few friends who, like himself, only enjoy high play, drop in for it whenever they feel inclined. Care to have a look in there? We'll slip away for half an hour."

They got their wraps, and sped quietly downstairs.

A word to her chauffeur, and Ann's car drew up at a house of flats in Park Lane. "Grayham," was murmured to the night porter on duty, and they were shown to a lift. Upstairs, on the top floor, their guide rang a certain bell and then disappeared.

The door was opened by a footman who evidently recognised Ann, for he led them down a short, broad corridor and opened a door at the end. The two stepped into a large, closely-curtained room in which chemin de fer and baccarat were in full swing.

There were no introductions. A tall, alert-faced man, rather of the army type, just glanced up, bowed to Ann, and went on dealing. No one else looked up at all.

Ann steered Violet to a small table in a bay window presided over by a very tall, very broad-shouldered, very muscular-looking servant.

"You take as many cardboard counters as you like," she explained lightly. "The man stamps your name on each, for they're as good as notes, and any which you don't use you yourself tear up.

It's only the ones you hand over that count as actual money. Those of this colour represent each five pounds; those, ten; those, fifty; those, one hundred. One-pound tokens? Oh, those lilac-coloured? But, of course, they're very seldom used here."

Violet helped herself well. She was feeling rich tonight. She would be married this time next week, and Arthur had had very generous settlements drawn up. She would be a very wealthy woman in a few days now. And, although Arthur's solicitors had stipulated in the settlements that he would not be responsible for any debts incurred by her before their marriage, Violet could smile at the stipulation. He was her abject slave, and he would remain so, she knew.

She glanced at the clock. It was just past midnight as she seated herself at the baccarat table. At first her luck was in. But it deserted her presently. By that time it was three o'clock in the morning, and Ann and she must return. Violet, however, found this easier said than done. Mr. Grayham and a couple of "friends" of his, at least, he called them so, moved incessantly to and fro, entering in their note-books how much each departing visitor owed, or was owed. Paying or receiving, accordingly, as swiftly as bank clerks. Mr. Grayham now came over to Violet, to whom he was introduced by Ann. Smiling genially, he said how much he regretted that Miss Finch's first visit had resulted in a deficit. Just a little matter of only four hundred and seventy-five pounds, however.

"A—a cheque "Violet said hastily—abruptly. "I'll draw you a cheque for it."

"Delighted," murmured her host. "In this side-room." He held open its door and the three stepped in. Shutting the door behind him, he motioned the two young women to a writing-table and comfortable arm-chairs.

"I'll leave you while you draw it," he murmured. Then he added as in afterthought, "By the way, I hope you don't mind, but as this is your guest's first visit, Miss Lovelace, will you write me a line as sponsor for the cheque? You know our few rules."

"Certainly," Ann replied carelessly, and Mr. Grayham left them.

Ann adjusted the pale pastel flowers that formed one of her shoulder straps, and with which her cloak of silver cloth seemed lined. Violet drew a deep breath as she picked up a pen.

"Of course, I can't guarantee your cheque without any security for it," Ann said smilingly. "But if you're in a tight hole for the moment I'll lend you the money with pleasure."

"Oh, will you?" Violet's tone was effusively grateful.

"Certainly. On the shorter of your two pearl necklaces so gorgeously displayed around your pretty throat. As I helped you choose it, I don't need to have it valued first. Just over a thousand pounds Arthur paid for it, I know. You're a lucky girl, Violet. Well, would you like me to give Grayham my cheque instead of drawing one yourself?"

"Oh, thanks ever so!" Violet unfastened the string of lovely pearls in question and stood playing with it, running the pearls fondly through her well-manicured rather thick fingers, while Ann, picking up a pen, drew her cheque for the four hundred and seventy-five pounds. But, as Violet handed the pearls to her, Ann asked her to sit down again for a moment more.

"You must give me a line, you know, to say that the pearls are one of the two strings I saw bought, the 'Queen Charlotte's pearls,' as they were called by the jeweller; and a further line to say that they are your own property, that you have a perfect right to raise a loan on them, and that you will redeem them within a month after your marriage to Arthur, at latest."

"But surely all that's quite unnecessary between friends, as we are," Violet exclaimed, with a confident smile.

"Absolutely necessary," was the cool and quite definite reply. "To me, at least."

Violet met Ann's firm look and capitulated, though with an inward curse. She wrote the words dictated, signed the paper, handed it and the pearls to Ann, and received in return the cheque; then they stepped back into the other room. Mr. Grayham seemed to have eyes in the back of his head. He left one of his friends to continue paying out notes, and was at their side in a moment. Violet handed him Ann's cheque.

"Miss Finch will settle with me," Ann said lightly.

Grayham gave her a receipt, and saw them to the door, all smiles and pleasant speeches.

At eleven next morning, Arthur was told that Miss Lovelace and Miss Walsh had called and would like to see him.

The drawing-room in Grosvenor Square looked very pleasant that sunny morning, but it was unmistakably the drawing-room of a bachelor—or a widower. Arthur's mother had died at his birth.

"Kitty, what's the matter?" Arthur began, before he was well into the room.

Kitty shook her head. She looked uneasy. "Don't ask me. This is Ann's show. She routed me out this morning and said I must come along. That it was a family matter—a 'Walsh ' matter."

Ann Lovelace—dressed in cool-looking muslin and a large, shady black hat—hesitated a moment perceptibly.

Her long gloves, matching her bag and shoes, were black, and she stood smoothing them along her slender arms before she spoke.

"It's a very serious matter, I fear," she said at length, hesitantly. "And I hate to speak of it, Arthur. Believe me, I do, indeed, but I can't help myself. It's concerned with Violet Finch."

"Then she ought to be present," Kitty broke in hotly.

Ann silenced her with a look—calm, but authoritative. "Not at all! On the contrary, we must first decide what is best to be done for all sakes. She borrowed close on five hundred pounds from me last night. Oh–" in reply to a quick forward step on Arthur's part. "It's not the money that troubles me! But she asked me to lend it to her on the security of one of those pearl necklaces you had given her. One of the 'Queen Charlotte's' necklaces. I agreed, and suggested the smaller one." She paused.

"Well?" snapped Arthur. His face had flushed deeply. Even the whites of his eyes were suffused.

Kitty was speechless. What was coming? If she knew Ann—and she did—it would be something very clever—and very unpleasant for Violet Finch. For that Ann Lovelace was no friend of Arthur's fiancée, Kitty was convinced.

With great deliberation Ann undid her black shopping bag with its chased silver mount to let her slender, coral-nailed fingers extract a string of pearls and a sheet of note-paper. "Here is what she wrote, assuring me that these pearls are her own property, and that she has therefore a perfect right to raise a loan on them. Well, by merest chance, as it happens, I heard this morning that the pearls are not at all Violet's as yet. That they are only to become her own on her wedding day; and that even then they are to be family heirlooms. Which means, of course, that she had absolutely no right whatever to pledge them to me for the requested loan."

"I will make that pledge good," Arthur declared instantly and stiffly; and Kitty could have clapped him on the shoulder for the championship, for his deep and loyal anger at the aspersion against Violet.

"Yes, I don't doubt that you would," Ann said gently. "But I don't see how we're going to get around a startling difficulty in the way. These pearls aren't real. This is a necklace of imitation pearls."

"Nonsense!" Arthur exclaimed rudely, furiously, while Kitty caught her breath in, aghast.

Violet had certainly had no shadow of right to allege—as she had in that paper; it lay on the table and Kitty was reading it—that she owned the pearls; but that was as nothing to this dreadful rider. In a few days the pearls given to Violet provisionally were to be truly her own, as Arthur's wedding gift, although to be held as an heirloom. But if there were any reality in Ann's accusation!

"You're talking nonsense, and spiteful nonsense!" Arthur went on still more roughly. "Of course these are the pearls I bought as part of my wedding gift."

He reached out to seize them, but in a twinkling Ann had slipped the string over her head and down inside her frock. She had on an ostrich-feather boa, and it covered the clasp.

"It's a lie!" Arthur exclaimed with clenching teeth, looking as though he could have struck Violet's accuser.

"Arthur!" Ann said quietly, "I think you're growing a bit Finchy yourself. J don't tell lies, nor cheat, nor steal. For that so-called ' loan ' was stolen from me. I've asked Violet to meet me here without fail; and, as I hear some car driving up in a great hurry, it's probably hers. Oh, I haven't any wish to take her character away behind her back!" she finished with an open sneer. "I tried to get the Colonel here, too; but he couldn't come."

The rage in Arthur's face again did Kitty good to see. But its occasion was tragic. If Ann's charge had any foundation . . .! Could it possibly have any? Ann was a serpent. . . . Guile was her positive genius. . . .

Quick and not overlight feet could now be heard coming up the stairs, and Violet was shown in. Was it that Kitty's eye was distorted by the previous scene? Or did Violet usually dress with greater care? Look less— well, yes, less common?

"What's it all about?" Violet demanded, as she entered, her colour mounting and then paling sickeningly as she saw Ann Lovelace. Kitty did not like that whitening face.

"Miss Finch, you got me to lend you close on five hundred pounds on a sham security," Ann said clearly and haughtily. "These aren't pearls at all. They're wax beads."

Kitty gave a sort of cry at this, and snatched in her turn at the string around Ann's neck which the wearer was touching scornfully.

"You liar! Or you've changed them!" Violet said hoarsely. And, as she heard her, a great relief came to Kitty. Of course! Ann had dug a pit, and was now about to fall into it herself. Kitty had never before known Ann to go anything like as far as this. But, given sufficient motive—and cover—there was nothing sinister of which she believed her incapable.

"Ah!" came from Arthur. And his tone of relief told Kitty how similarly he had been feeling. "Ah, I might have thought of that!"

"Instead of believing her lies against me!" stormed Violet.

"I didn't believe them, darling," he said swiftly. "But neither did I dream of such an explanation."

"Not being an absolute fool, you didn't," Ann interrupted, for hate was rising above dignified coolness. "How could I have had pearls copied which were not in my possession? If you weigh this string and the real one— if you even lay them side by side—you'll find them apparently identical. I've been to Rinks' this morning with that string, and they looked up their books."

Here Violet grew abusive, shrilling out her version of the affair. On Ann's insistence she had handed her the real pearls last night and regretted it bitterly enough at

the time. She clutched Arthur's arm and assured him
that she would never, never, never touch a gambling card
again. She shrieked at Ann's perfidy in having taken her
to a private gambling place for her own ends.

Kitty had never admired Arthur so much as now. It
was both pain and pleasure to see how his hand covered
Violet's, how he held her close, how he soothed and tried
to quiet her hysterical rage.

And in the end Ann was beaten. Kitty had never
hoped for this. But Arthur refused to listen to her, and as
Ann, forgetting other things for the moment, leant far
forward to assure Arthur that he was making the mistake
of his life in not believing her, the beads swung free from
her hands, and in a second, with a swiftness and a force
that delighted Kitty, though it startled her, Violet had
grabbed them, tugged the string in two, though it was
strongly knotted between each pearl, and thrust them
into the little silk handbag that she clutched tightly
under her arm.

For a second Kitty thought Ann would actually spring
at the other girl. But her self-control held. Instead, she
gave Violet a look of such real and utter contempt that
Kitty's faith wavered, gave Arthur its mate, and then,
head high, would have left the room had not Arthur
placed himself with his back to the door to prevent it.

"No, you can't leave like that, Ann," he said, and
spoke in measured tones. "Not until you fully realise that
if one word of these false accusations of yours get about I
shall bring an action for libel—or rather my wife will."

Ann looked about her for the paper that had lain on
the table. It, too, was gone—into Arthur Walsh's pocket!

"You have no proofs!" His flaming eyes burnt out of
his deeply-flushed face as he spoke. He was in a rage of
which Kitty had never thought him capable.

"Here is my cheque for your loan. I insist on your
taking it. Violet regrets the whole transaction deeply.
That, instead of coming to me, she borrowed from you.
But your tale about her having got the loan from you on

imitation pearls "His teeth clicked together audibly. The muscles on his cheeks bulged for a second. Again Kitty felt that the natural man would have liked to hit out at Ann, standing quite composedly, though very white, before him.

For a second they stood face to face, then she made a gesture with her hand, motioning him to step out of her way. But he held his ground.

"I must have your promise, Ann, to keep absolute silence about this whole scene and affair," he persisted. "You thought you could disgrace Violet. You planned it all with devilish cleverness. But it won't work. I believe she speaks the truth, and I don't believe that you do, about the whole miserable matter."

"Yet you carefully pocket the paper she signed?" Ann's voice was contemptuous.

He nodded.

"And she broke and pocketed the string of alleged pearls!"

For a second Ann's self-control shook again, but she said no more, only stood a moment with head bent. Then she raised it to add quietly:

"I thought you were making a dreadful mistake. But it seems that it was I who made one. I see now that you and Miss Finch are well matched. As for your cheque repaying me, I accept it. I have no intention whatever—though she had—of making your fiancée a present of my loan." Her tone was steel. Then she stopped herself and with a final gesture of utter scorn for both, passed through the door which he now held open for her departure.

"Darling!" Violet flung her arms around Arthur's neck. "My own darling! That hateful creature! What awful lies! Oh, take me away, where I shall never meet her again!"

"My own Violet!" Arthur said tenderly. "I'll take you home at once. Forget the whole spiteful fiasco! But what about you, Kit? Will you come, too?"

Kitty, however, promptly said she needed a walk. And she did. A silent, almost forgotten spectator of the drama, she felt her brain spinning as she recalled it. What would her uncle do? Would he try to stop the marriage by cutting off Arthur's hugely increased marriage allowance and revoking his gift of the capital involved? As well as that of the Town house? Kitty wondered sadly if a struggle were coming between the Colonel and this his second and only surviving son? For Arthur would not give Violet up—of that Kitty now felt sure. But what would her uncle's attitude be? He was a broad-minded man, with but one detestation—personal deceit, and especially of a lie to him. That had cost him Gerald. Was it now — through Violet Finch—to cost him Arthur? For Violet had set it down in black and white that the pledged pearls were her actual property. . . .

Kitty thought that Violet might have considered that a very trifling inaccuracy; but to her uncle there was no such thing as a "trifling" untruth. And, apart from that, even for Violet Finch it was surely no mere inaccuracy to say that wax imitations were real pearls, and to borrow a considerable sum of money on them. . . . Kitty felt that she must get some clear idea of what had really happened. She could not discuss it with her uncle. Arthur might, but Kitty carried no guns that could cope with her uncle's. Then she bethought herself of Ambrose Walsh, her cousin and Arthur's.

Ambrose Walsh was a priest. He was only a little older than Arthur himself, but brilliant, even as a boy. You never could deceive Ambrose in the old days; and he was hardly likely to have grown less clear-sighted with the years. He was home, from a leper station, on sick leave, which he was using to write a book. His few books were by way of being literary landmarks.

Kitty had always liked Ambrose. Fearless, honest, by character he might have been Colonel Walsh's son instead of his nephew. She would try for an interview with him in private. She had better telephone first and find out if he could see her. For Father Walsh was an important person. The lay brother who answered the telephone asked her name. He told her that Father Walsh was engaged for the moment and had an appointment for the next hour, but if Miss Walsh could come then . . .? Kitty could and would. She felt chilled at the thought of even the hour's delay, and half regretted the impulse that had made her ring her cousin up. But, having done so, she must keep the appointment.

Chapter Four: A Marriage Takes Place

Kitty was before her time at the Priest's House in Islington. She was shown into a very bare little waiting-room. Three doors opened out of it. One was Ambrose Walsh's sitting-room, and she heard voices in conversation within it. Kitty stiffened, for one voice was Ann's. Well, she might have known it. Ambrose had been Ann's confessor for a few months. Ann would be sure to want to get her story in first. Very likely she was even enlisting Ambrose's help to give the Colonel her version of what had happened. What had happened? Kitty asked herself again. Who had been lying . . .? Something about Ann's exit had been very telling. . . . And, though it seemed incredible that Violet should have done such a thing, yet how had the pearls been imitated?

But against those doubts rose her old well-founded distrust of Ann Lovelace. Ann of the quiet voice and effective manner, the cool calm eyes, the subtle brain. Kitty had felt quite certain that Ann meant to get triumphantly between Arthur and Violet Finch, that she had secretly tried hard to do this during the week they had all spent together at the Walsh's place in the country.

For when Arthur wrote that he was bringing his fiancee down for a week's visit, his aunt had promptly asked Ann to come down, too. Ann, with whom Arthur had been so madly in love, in the days when Gerald was still at home. Handsome, careless, undependable Gerald. The days when Arthur, though well off, was still only the younger son. There was no entail in the family. The Colonel could leave his really big fortune as he liked, but it was natural to expect that the elder would get the lion's share. Also, Ann, at that time, was all out to marry Lord

Wilverstone. But there, too, she failed. Lord Wilverstone married an old love of his, despite Ann's cleverest counter-diplomacy. Kitty happened to know, however, that Ann had nearly succeeded there.

Again her thoughts returned, now, to her present problem, as she distantly heard the sound of Ann Lovelace's quiet but "carrying" voice, speaking evidently with what, for Ann, amounted to vehemence. Nor were the sounds misleading. For, inside, Father Ambrose and Ann were facing each other dynamically at the two ends of his mantelshelf. The Reverend Ambrose Walsh was solidly built, physically, and something about his face, with its strongly-marked features, suggested a character also firmly built. Pale of face, with a beak of a nose, a flexible, long upper lip and firm jaw—his brilliant and keenly-penetrating eyes were fastened searchingly on his visitor's.

"It's a bad, sad business," he said regretfully when she stepped speaking. His own voice had irrepressible warm undertones. It suggested subdued but strong passions underneath. Just as his face did. "A very bad, very sad business," he repeated, half to himself. "But if it breaks his engagement to such a character it may prove a blessing to him yet."

"It won't break it!" Ann said decisively. "Nothing can do that. It's as if she had Arthur under a witch's spell."

"I wonder what his father, my uncle, will say," murmured Ambrose Walsh reflectively.

"Oh, Arthur will swear to him by all his gods that Violet's an innocent dove, that it's I, not she, that is the guilty one."

A very penetrating glance flashed for a second from Father Ambrose's eyes, but Ann's were fastened on her gloves, as she wrinkled and smoothed their gauntlets. "He once trusted and liked me," she continued composedly; "but Violet Finch holds him, as I said, just as though he were under some spell. He can't seem to see or hear the truth, where she's concerned. You met her, I remember, one afternoon down at Friar's Halt. Did you see anything in her to account for such an infatuation?"

The priest made no answer and Ann moved towards the door.

"I wanted you to know all the facts, Father, so as to be able to explain things to your uncle, Colonel Walsh." Ann had not come for that reason at all. But she knew that Ambrose Walsh was against the marriage; and she hoped that, learning from her what more than sufficient reason he had for his opposition—he would increase his personal pressure on Arthur to persuade him to give up the girl. After all, Arthur, too, was a Catholic. Like all the Walshes, at one time, he had been quite under his cousin's influence.

Father Ambrose showed her out by a door that did not lead back into the common sitting-room where Kitty sat impatiently counting the minutes. Then he gravely welcomed his second visitor. His eyes lit up as they shook hands, for he liked Kitty sincerely. And whenever he saw her he saw not the charming young woman, but his romping child cousin. Saw himself, too, again a mischievous schoolboy making her walk the plank into a tub of water and getting soundly thrashed for it afterwards, as well as in a score of childhood's scenes.

He led her into his own little sitting-room and closed the door. "Well, Kit? What brings you for the first time to see me here?"

"I oughtn't to have come," she said to that. "Really, Ambrose, I shouldn't take up your time, but I'm bewildered . . . and frightened. Ann Lovelace has just left, hasn't she? Oh, never mind," as he made no reply. "I know she has been here. I'm come on the same matter. . . . That accusation against Violet Finch about the pearls—"

"You don't think the charge of fraud is true?" he questioned.

"No, I don't," she replied promptly. "Partly because Ann Lovelace is making it, and also because it's absolutely incredible! It makes Arthur's fiancee just a common thief!"

"Nevertheless, it would be the best thing that could happen to Arthur if it could be shown to be true," Ambrose said in his authoritative, crisp way. "I didn't say that to Ann, and I shan't say it to Arthur, probably. But it's stern facts, Kit. I have met Miss Finch, have talked with her, studied her. And I tell you candidly—and confidentially—that if Arthur marries her—he's doomed!"

"Why!—" Kitty demanded. But she knew how uncannily right Ambrose's summing up of people and consequences used to prove in the end.

"Because she's devoted, soul and body, to the World and the Flesh—if not to the Devil. And because Arthur is only too much inclined that way himself."

"You always wanted Arthur to be a priest, too!" Kitty said resentfully.

He gave her a steely look. "Catherine"—Ambrose only called her that when he wished to emphasise the fact that he was speaking with authority—" stand aside! Have nothing to do with the woman or the affair of her pearls. It is just possible that Providence may be going to take a hand—to save Arthur from damnation."

"Marriage with Violet Finch doesn't mean damnation—necessarily," she protested indignantly. "I wish, of course, that she were one of us. But she may come to be—given time and fair play."

Ambrose looked very much the priest. His face stiffened, his look grew inscrutable. He was clearly not taken with the notion of a converted Violet.

There was a short silence. Kitty felt done. She had come for nothing. Ambrose had no light to shed on this matter. Or if he had, he was keeping it for his own use. But she stood to her guns.

"Ambrose, Ann, of course, has told you her version—"

"I think she's told me the truth," he said deliberately, dispassionately. "I questioned her closely."

"I don't think she has!" Kitty blazed out. "Not by a long, long lot! Ann Lovelace would do anything to get her knife into Violet, to get Arthur from her—for herself!"

Her cousin, Ambrose, seemed, on this, to have grown very chilling, very distant, as he looked down at her with eyes veiled and inscrutable.

"At least, whatever may be her faults, she is a lady and a religious woman at heart," he answered sternly.

"Oh, stuff, Ambrose!" Kitty said hotly, throwing off the awe of the priest. "That's her cloak. She's just a—" But she stopped herself. For the Reverend Ambrose Walsh did not seem to hear her. She recognised clearly that his mind was definitely closed to any further discussion of Violet's case.

"Evidently you're on Ann's side," she concluded coldly.

And at that Father Ambrose gave a fleeting smile as he said calmly, "I'm on her side, certainly, if she can rightly prevent Arthur's disastrous marriage to Miss Finch."

Kitty rose to leave. Coldly asking, as she glanced at his writing-table overflowing with papers and books: "What is your coming book about?"

"The Church Militant," he said in a ringing tone. "There's far too much talk of converts slithering from the Anglican Church into ours as though there were small difference between them. I want the gates, on the contrary, to be barred and locked, except to those who show the right credentials for admission. I want there to be an end to marriages between ourselves and heretics— no matter though we do get their children, who are not worth the having, as a rule.

"I would rather—" He stopped himself. To Ambrose Walsh the sheep and the goats were born to be separated. And only he himself knew what a blow it had been to him to learn that his cousin Arthur was going to marry outside his Church, even apart from other considerations. There had been a time when he had seen a great deal of Arthur . . . when he had cherished strong hopes of getting him, too, to enter a Religious Life, either as a Priest or as a Brother. But in these last years Arthur had drawn away more and more from Ambrose, had left his letters unanswered, had refused to be in when he called. . . . To any one who knew Ambrose Walsh at all, Arthur could have done nothing better calculated to make his cousin more firmly determined on getting his own way—even had there been no religious dynamic involved.

In silence he opened the door now for Kitty's departure; and she felt herself still in pinafores, morally, as she said good-bye to him. She went down at once to Friar's Halt, and saw, as she stepped into Colonel Walsh's study, that he knew. He looked as though he had had a great shock.

"You've seen Ann," she said without hesitation.

He nodded. "She met me going to my club."

He paused as Arthur came hurrying into the house and the room. He had driven Violet home, and had had a hard task to convince her that to him she was beyond suspicion, far above reproach. But he had succeeded in doing so. Now, as soon as he saw his father's face, he, too, knew that the Colonel had been met by Ann and her story.

His own face hardened; his back straightened; his jaw set.

"I'd like you to stay, Kitty," was his greeting, "as Violet's friend. Thank God, you're not prejudiced against her!"

"No, I'm not," Kitty replied. Hearing which, the Colonel wheeled on her.

"What? You don't believe—?" He checked himself. "Look here," he began again, "I don't think we need drag you into this harrowing question, Kitty, except for one vital query. Have you ever known Ann Lovelace to tell a lie? I don't mean those polite, stereotyped words which we all use as 'delighted' to meet people, or 'sorry' to see them go, etcetera. I mean by a ' lie ' a deliberate, downright falsehood. Have you ever heard her utter one?"

"No," Kitty answered reluctantly. "But I've known her do still worse when it suited her game. I've known her so to put the truth so that it sounded more false than any outright lie could be."

"Oh, quite possible," agreed the Colonel promptly. "But subtlety of that sort need not be considered here, even if a fact. For here Ann makes certain definite assertions. She declares that she lent a considerable sum of money to Miss Finch on the pledged security of a certain necklace which was not, as Miss Finch stated them to be, her own property, and which, moreover, is not a string of real pearls, but a wax imitation. Ann and I went to Rinks', and saw the assistant manager who dealt with the affair. He assured me that the necklace shown him by Miss Lovelace earlier this morning was an exact facsimile of the shorter of the two necklaces which you, Arthur, bought of them.

"He agreed, too, with Ann that such a copy could only have been made from the original; and then only by an expert craftsman. He also further affirmed that the imitation Ann showed him was an exact duplicate of the original pearl necklace in weight and colour. For Ann had made him go into the matter very thoroughly indeed before coming to you, Arthur.

"Now, my boy, I'm inexpressibly sorry for your terrible shock; but I can't see that there's any possibility that Ann is not telling the absolute truth about it. She says you have taken possession of the paper written by Violet herself—"At this point Colonel Walsh caught sight of aghast Kitty, and insisted on her leaving them. He had quite forgotten her presence. And this was no question of attitude to one or the other girl. It was a question of actual facts; and the Colonel uncompromisingly held that he and his only son must sift these to the bottom together.

Kitty glanced back at her cousin. He looked like a man bracing himself for a bitter struggle, but firmly determined not to yield an inch of ground. And something in her leapt to meet this new Arthur, while her heart seemed a stricken thing.

As the door closed behind her, there was a second's silence, then Arthur said: "I have just given Violet those pearls outright, sir, though they will still be my wedding present to her. So she has a perfect right to raise money on them in such a position as she found herself in last night; a position, too, into which she had been jockeyed by Ann. Violet had no other way of paying her gaming debt there and then. And, seeing that clearly, she took it. Ann had grossly deceived her as to the value of the discs with which they were playing. She had told her that they represented shillings, whereas they were pounds. Violet's no practised gambler, sir."

"Even though her mother had long kept what were essentially gambling hells?" the Colonel asked gently, for he was desperately sorry for his unhappy son.

"Just because of that, sir," Arthur said soberly. "I didn't conceal from you that, had I known beforehand whose daughter she was, I wouldn't have avoided her. But as it was . . . and is . . . she's the only woman in the world for me. She's quite incapable of the charge against her." He stopped. Arthur was never given to long speeches.

His father's eyes were unrelenting, although his voice had real compunction in its tones.

"Sorry, my dear boy; but after what has come indubitably to light there can be no going on with the wedding. Surely you must see that, too?"

"I surely do not, sir!" Arthur's tones were no less firm than his father's. "It's a vile plot, Ann Lovelace's plot against Violet. I won't let her, or any one, come between me and the girl I love! Violet's as true as steel. Honest, loyal, honourable. Without a crooked fibre in her."

"She lied deliberately when she pledged those pearls as her own property," the Colonel said in a grim voice. "No, no"—as Arthur made a violent movement. "That's not all by a long way. But it is a thing to which you can't shut your eyes. Ann didn't write that I.O.U. Miss Finch wrote it herself, alleging both that she owned the pearls and that the string which she was handing over to Ann as security for the loan was one of the two that Ann had helped her choose and seen taken. The value of which Ann could therefore take on trust. And I cannot see any loophole where Miss Finch wasn't lying about that last, too."

Arthur kept silent with an effort; but he looked furious and obstinate.

"You know," the Colonel went on, "what I feel about a lie. It's not prejudice. It's not attaching an exaggerated importance to something that really means very little. All civilisation, all intercourse, all business, is built up on the belief that you can rely on a deliberate assertion. Why, Religion itself depends on that! I cut your brother Gerald off as I did because he was a deliberate liar; in other words, a moral leper. Do you mean to tell me that you intend to choose such a leper for your wife? For the mother of your children?"

"I maintain that it is Ann who is the 'moral leper ' here," Arthur said hotly. "I deny absolutely that Violet was lying when she scribbled down those words about being the owner of the pearls. I had told her yesterday that they would be hers—absolutely—on her wedding day. As for the effective use that Ann made of an imitation necklace on which to base her accusations against Violet, I intend to have that curiously plausible production drastically investigated, you may rest assured, Pater! And you may also rest assured that my wife's honour will be irrefutably vindicated," Arthur's voice rang out. And like Kitty, his father rated him the higher for his unshakable and impassioned championship of the girl he loved. Yet Colonel Walsh was no less convinced that his son was the victim of a sheer infatuation.

"Love is often blind," he said gravely.

"I'm not blind!" Arthur exclaimed hotly. "Ann Lovelace hasn't succeeded in pulling her unscrupulously clever wool over my eyes, as she has, apparently, over yours, sir."

The Colonel took it quietly. He was too sorry for his son, too certain that he would yet know the bitterness of awaking, to be angry.

"How do you mean to prove your case?" he asked, "since you intend to do so?"

"I mean to hand the whole thing over to a first-class private investigator," was the firm reply.

"That's sensible!" The Colonel looked, and was relieved. But he was sorrier still for Arthur. "I think you'd better let me see about that," he said a little awkwardly.

Arthur's eyes flashed. "You can call in your own man, too, sir, if you like. But I claim the right to be first in the field. There's only one thing I do insist on. No steps must be taken openly for at least a fortnight. Vi and I believe that this is the only way to give my detective a chance to get at the root and branches of the matter. I'm keen to have Victor Sewell take charge of the investigation for me, and his secretary has told me, over the phone, that Sewell won't be back in town for another ten days. So everything must be at a standstill until then."

"Victor Sewell?" the colonel asked. "Never heard of him. Who is he?"

"He's studied for the Bar, but he's private means and likes problems. Just now he's clearing up a very private and difficult matter at Oxford in which two college men are concerned," Arthur replied. "That's in strict confidence, you know. He's a member of White's. Incidentally, he's a son of the former Commissioner of New Scotland Yard."

"Of that Sewell? Clever chap, the old general. Well, if you think he can serve you in this sad affair—"The colonel looked very pityingly at Arthur standing there before him all fire and eagerness.

"He'll clear Vi, sir," the younger man spoke with a certainty in his voice and face that made the father's heart ache for him. "He'll find out the truth. But till then,

Vi's to have fair treatment from everybody. I'll put the fear of God into Ann if she starts letting her tongue run away with her."

"Ann's tongue doesn't run loosely," the colonel said dryly to that; "but I think I may possibly be able to persuade her to an active truce. What about the insurance, though? Are you notifying them that the smaller string seems lost?"

"Not just yet," Arthur said. "Both strings were insured up to the hilt, of course. But Vi thinks that, if Ann does not suspect us of setting investigations and detectives at work, her clever wits will devise some way to plausibly return the real pearls.

"Vi's a marvel, sir!" his son ejaculated. "Most girls, under such an abominable charge, would be wanting Ann Lovelace's blood. Yet Vi actually believes that Ann may have somehow been 'had' too! I think she suspects her mother's partner, Mills, of having had some hand in the exchange. But I, myself, don't agree there. I used to know Mills rather well, at one time. It was he who introduced me to the Little Owls. They were top-hole in those days— I can't think Mills would have a hand in such an injury to Violet. I used to be no end of jealous of him at first. I thought Vi liked him best. However ... no open move to be made until Sewell takes the reins, to drive the whole thing straight to the truth."

Colonel Walsh responded hopefully outwardly, but with a sickening certainty that Arthur was riding for a terrible fall. He went up to Town to see Ann, though, and found her not so easy to deal with as he had hoped. In the end, however, he got her promise to keep the whole affair absolutely to herself at present. But he left her more than ever persuaded that she was sincere and had really been duped by Violet Finch. Nevertheless, it seemed to him odd that Ann—familiar with valuable pearls— should not have instantly detected the "feel" of imitation pearls when they were handed over to her.

This was on Wednesday. And on the following Saturday the colonel received a terrible blow. It was a letter from Arthur delivered by hand. In this his son stated that he had been married to Violet Finch that morning at the Kingsway registry office; and that they were on a flying " honeymoonette" in the Engadine. They would be "back home on Tuesday next."

The Colonel sat very still. At first he felt as though he had heard that Arthur had flung himself over a precipice. Then common sense came to his aid. After all, marriages nowadays were anything but permanent. . . . And even did this one prove so, he must hope for the best. There must be something sweet in Violet to account for Arthur's indomitable devotion. And with sweetness allied to spirit no wife could be a misfortune.

Kitty was away from home and he was glad that she, too, would be gone until Tuesday. In reality she was back on Monday; and the colonel told himself thankfully that he must have been mistaken in thinking that she had secretly given her heart to Arthur. For when she learnt the news Kitty took Arthur's part against his aunt; who could not forgive him "his mad marriage to Violet Finch!"

"You should cut him off! You did Gerald for far less!" Lady Monkhouse said furiously to her brother.

Colonel Walsh winced, but he replied quietly: "Arthur has a perfect right to follow the dictates of his heart. He did not deceive me. I may agree that he is a besotted, if not hoodwinked, young fool; but that's no reason for attempting to make him see things as we do. Arthur is deeply in love with Violet, my dear. I only hope he may prove to be right about her, may be able to stay in love with her always. As to my Deed of Gift on his marriage, it was executed a week ago; and so comes into
operation at once."

His sister snorted, but the colonel continued calmly: "He writes that they are going to stay in Mrs. Finch's house in Ennismore Gardens, when they get back, until the house in Grosvenor Square can be redecorated"

"It didn't need any redecorating," snapped his sister; "but I don't doubt that Finch woman needs the money. He'll pay her for the use of hers."

The colonel said no more. He was lunching with Ambrose and feared that he must listen to similar sentiments about the marriage. But his nephew offered no comment beyond the significant priestly aphorism that "God's ways are not our ways. Neither are the devil's, unless we serve him."

CHAPTER FIVE: A PRIVATE INVESTIGATOR IS CALLED IN

The wedding had been a very quiet one, even for a registry office. Mrs. Finch, who had been away with Mills superintending the sale of one of her Maidenhead clubs, came up for it—after she had ascertained from her solicitors that the settlements had been duly signed. Besides which preliminary she had seen to it that both bridegroom and bride executed each a will. Arthur's bequeathing to Violet everything of which he should die possessed or entitled to; and Violet's bequeathing similarly everything to her mother, Mrs. Finch-Gray.

Only when these matters were all to her satisfaction did "Mrs. Finch" instruct Ronald Mills—who had motored her up to town—to fetch from their car her wedding present to her new-made son-in-law. As she presented it, she said apologetically:

"You insisted on such an unexpectedly sudden marriage, my dear Arthur, that I was only able to lay my hands on what I hope may prove useful." Adding sardonically, as she could not ignore his blank look at the small picnic hamper for two which she held out smilingly to him: "The wine is good and I made the sandwiches myself."

Arthur perforce thanked her, promptly transferred the contents of the little hamper to his suitcase, throwing the wickerwork away. Violet was quite incapable of dealing with even such small incidentals to her hasty wedding. She looked almost drunk with joy as she kissed her mother and shook hands with Ronald Mills and jumped laughingly, with Arthur's fond help, into the car waiting to take them to Croydon Aerodrome.

On Tuesday they were back again. Mrs. Finch was still down at Maidenhead with Mills, but the servants at the house in Ennismore Gardens had everything ready for the young couple.

After many kisses, Arthur left Violet and went to hunt up Victor Sewell at the latter's smart office at Buckingham Gardens. He had assured Violet that he would do this the first moment they were back in town.

Violet had not shown any impatience about it, but Arthur had referred again and again to the situation as intolerable, one which must be cleared up immediately, quite irrespective of the loss of the necklace. He assured Violet over and over again that she was not to worry, that Sewell would see to it that the whole truth came out.

It was with a very lack-lustre eye that his young bride thanked him. Violet, in truth, had quite lost the exultantly rapturous look she had worn at her wedding. Indeed her whole expression as she watched the cliffs of England show white below them, and then the growing green of the trees and the silver sheen of the Thames, looked as though she were nerving herself to face trouble.

Arthur noticed it and pressed her hand. "Don't worry, darling," he said in her ear, making an excuse of getting up to look down at something below them. "Sewell has keen brains. He'll dig out the truth."

But Violet swallowed something in her throat as she returned his caress.

On calling, Arthur was shown at once into Victor Sewell's professional office. A spacious but somewhat bare-looking room, with a pair of comfortable arm-chairs, a knee-hole writing-table, and very little else—that could be seen. For its microphones and wall cameras were well concealed. But these latter were not wanted now. Sewell knew and liked Arthur Walsh. Apart from that, he was glad to be called in by him, for Colonel Walsh's circle of friends included all the most influential names in the British world of big finance.

Sewell himself was quite well off, but he had a liking for investigation and was determined to make it a successful business. He called himself a "Clearing Agent" because he would only take defensive cases. Cases, that is, where he was engaged to clear the good name of some aspersed person.

In physique he rather suggested an intelligent monkey. He had a small dark face with a low forehead, crossed by innumerable deep lines. When thinking he would raise his eyebrows, wrinkling his forehead like a concertina, and gaze pensively at you from deep-set melancholy brown eyes. In his movements, too, he was quick and darting, as if mentally so. But his manner had remarkable charm. He would listen in absolute silence to any story; and yet, through his silence, by the eloquence of his eye he could, when he wished, encourage and calm. Nothing seemed to shock or even to surprise him.

Sewell was, as Arthur Walsh had informed his father, the son of a former Commissioner of New Scotland Yard; but he did not mean to rise by standing on his father's shoulders. Yet, should the Yard's help be needed in his investigations, he could rely on its doing all that it could to assist him. Sewell was not yet six-and-twenty, but looked much older; a point which he rightly regarded as an asset.

"Help yourself, my dear fellow," he said cordially to his visitor, pushing towards him a tray of choice cigars and cigarettes. And—confining his initial story to a bare relation of Ann Lovelace's charges and assertions about the affair to himself and to his father—Arthur paused there for Sewell's comments or questions. The first being: "The pearls are worth, intrinsically?"

To which his client replied by explaining in detail that on entering the famous jeweller's shop he had stated that he was looking for a handsome wedding present for his fiancee, and had been shown two necklace-strings of pearls, which had been the late Queen Charlotte's favourite wear. He had taken them both, paying five thousand pounds for the two; the smaller one, now in question, was priced around one thousand. His fiancee told him that she herself had insured them up to the hilt; the insurance to run from the date of their wedding.

"So she could prosecute, if need be?"

"Yes, but she says she won't," Arthur replied. "Women have queer reasonings, whether or not they are always intuitions. And I'm half inclined to share her suspicion that her mother's partner, Mills, is somehow at the bottom of the mystery. Though he was by way of being rather a friend of mine at one time. Ronald Mills—clever chap! Know him?"

"Just to speak to. A queer fish," Sewell said. "Nothing actually known against him, yet more than a little rumoured privately. But, of course, the devil of it is . . ." He hesitated; his brows working in embarrassed cogitation.

"You mean Mrs. Finch?" Arthur said at once. "That he's a sort of partner of hers? Or was. I believe they're winding up the Little Owls. But I'm not going to let that stand in the way of clearing my wife from any suspicion of doing a shady act. When you know her, Sewell, you'll realise how simply impossible it is to think of her as deceiving any one. But Miss Lovelace doesn't really know her at all. Hasn't discovered her true character. My cousin, Kitty Walsh—you know her, I think?"

"Rather!" Sewell said warmly.

"Well, she's on Violet's side. She knows her well, you see. And as to Mrs. Finch . . . half of what's said against her is tittle-tattle, when not lies. Jealousy of her one-time amazing success; complacent pleasure at her failure, now. Lots of people are like that, you know. Claw on to those who're rising; trample on them when they're down."

Sewell nodded.

"Besides, I haven't married Mrs. Finch," Arthur continued with a smile. "And as to her partnership with Mills—after all, she had to have some one in the swim to help her enterprise. And Mills, as we know, has a dashed plausible way with him when he chooses. While at one time he was hand in glove with plenty of the right sort."

"No need to spare Mills," Sewell said. "But when can I see Mrs. Walsh? I must have a talk with her, of course, before I can start in for your wife. And I'd like to. I only take the kind of case that clears people—as you know. And this looks likely to prove one compact of counter-psychologies. Unusually interesting but rather unusually hedged with difficulties."

"Plenty of psychology but not much subtlety about stealing a valuable string of pearls if it could be managed, I should have thought," objected Arthur Walsh, but added heartily how glad he was, and how glad his young wife would be, to have Sewell undertake her defence and complete vindication. Would Sewell come back to lunch with them, as his wife also hoped?

Sewell had quite expected this invitation and had kept himself free to accept it. Arthur accordingly drove him back with him. Violet had arranged for her cousin-in-law, Kitty Walsh, to also lunch with them. And Kitty was delighted to hear that Victor Sewell—whom she had often met and sincerely liked —was to ferret out the truth about the whole mystifying, unhappy affair of the fraudulent pearls.

Sitting on together after lunch, Sewell put a number of leading questions vital to his understanding of the case at issue. His young hostess wore the remaining larger necklace, so that he could judge for himself how fine its smaller mate must be.

Violet herself unexpectedly surpassed Sewell's expectations after all that he had heard confidentially whispered about his friend's "registry marriage." She was handsome, evidently full of vitality, and by no means wanting in brains. And although he thought her utterly without personal charm, Arthur was clearly of the opposite opinion on that point. Which, of course, was just as it should be. Indeed his patent adoration, though he tried not to let it show beyond conventional good taste, was almost pathetic as Violet ordered him about, though playfully. And Sewell was glad to see that whatever she said would be endorsed by Arthur, who, of course, was formally his employer.

"I understand that you left the original necklace lying overnight on your dressing-table," he jotted down in his notebook. "And your door was probably unlocked?"

Violet laughed outright. "But of course! I was at home, Mr. Sewell. In my mother's house."

"I forgot," he murmured mendaciously, and then asked the names of any guests in the house at the time.

Mills had been one, it appeared, but had left the second day after the purchase of the pearls. Quite long enough, Sewell and Arthur both thought, to get possession of the pearls and, supposing him to know a skilful craftsman, to have him make a copy of it.

"He had his man with him, I suppose?" Sewell asked.

"No. Ronald had had to let him go. He's badly hit by this crash, you know. He's even given up his service suite and taken a flat over one of Mr. Gray's garages. And for Ronald that means horrid discomfort!" Violet's lip curled scornfully. She had evidently small sympathy, if any, liking, for Ronald Mills.

"I have heard a whisper?" Sewell said discreetly.

"Shouted sub rosa," Violet laughed. "Mrs. Yerkes? Ronald hopes to announce his engagement any day now. She's got no end of money."

A little more desultory talk wound up the luncheon party for Sewell and he took his leave, frankly keen to "get to work." This, he proposed to himself, should be on Ronald Mills's footsteps, whom he quite expected to find qualifying for the criminal's place contrived for the then Miss Finch; if her unacknowledged but circumstantially indicated suspicions had any foundation in fact. The issue, however, must rest with the parties vitally concerned. As a rule, his cases were not permitted to get into the courts.

Kitty was booked for a dress fitting. Arthur had a very full afternoon ahead of him. Violet got him to promise that he would meet her at the Grosvenor Square House at six and see how the drawing-room walls looked. She waved to him from the window, and then turned away with a very eager, business-like face. She had till six to herself . . . Mills was with her mother. Her stepfather? She could not be sure where he was. Probably at the garage in George Street. So much the better. He never

bothered her. He never bothered any one. Mr. Gray's passion was engineering, and he was generally to be found with his mechanics.

Violet looked at her watch, waited five minutes, and then went to the telephone and rang up a Major Richards. Giving him the number of Mills's flat in Stanley Mews, Mayfair, she added directions as to how to find the address. "The door to the flats over the garage is around the corner from the garage itself," she said. "It's rarely locked, and I shall leave it so that you only have to push it open when you reach it at four o'clock sharp. You'll of course come prepared to 'complete'?" Apparently this question received a satisfactory reply, for she hung up and turned away—to find her mother standing in the doorway.

"Prepared to complete what?" Mrs. Finch asked, after a rather tepid kiss on both sides.

"Oh, just a little deal," Violet said quickly, "over a short-term leasehold. But I had no idea you were coming back to-day. How nice!"

"I'm off again at once," her mother responded, going to a cabinet by the window and unlocking it with a tiny key which she took from her purse. "I need some papers I left here," she explained as she put a bunch in her bag.

"Why didn't you send that lazy hound, Ronald?" Violet asked in an indifferent tone, but with a watchful eye. How much had her mother overheard? You never could tell—with her.

"Oh, he's got wind of some party Mrs. Yerkes is throwing, and is running round trying to get invited. Well, 'bye till Friday, Vi." And Mrs. Finch ran down the front steps and jumped into a luxurious-looking car.

CHAPTER SIX: ARTHUR WALSH GETS A VERY CURIOUS MESSAGE, AND SCOTLAND YARD IS SUMMONED TO A MURDER CASE

It was at five o'clock that Mrs. Finch's parlourmaid, when passing Violet's door, caught the click of a key being turned in a lock inside the room, and then of a drawer pulled open. That would be Violet's big wardrobe trunk, she decided. Violet would never open the room door when that trunk was unlocked, she had noticed, so, with a malicious grin on her pert face, the maid tapped on it.

"Would you like any tea, madam?" she asked through it solicitously. As on other occasions, there was no reply except the turning-on of water into the fitted basin. This was Violet's well-known little trick when she wanted to pretend that she had not heard the knocking. The maid did not venture to knock again. Had Mrs. Arthur Walsh wanted tea she would have ordered it. And with an amused smile at the vexation that she was sure that she had caused, Gwendolyn went on down to the servants' hall.

Some ten minutes later the front-door bell rang. Answering it, she found Ronald Mills on the doorstep. He had a latch-key and generally used it; but he had forgotten it, he explained.

"Is Mrs. Walsh in, Gwennie?" he asked. "If so, I'd like to welcome her home from her honeymoon."

"Yes, sir. She's up in her bedroom." The maid tripped upstairs to deliver the message, but came down again in a minute to say that Miss Violet, or rather Mrs. Walsh, must have just gone out. "She was in, I know, not ten minutes ago," she added.

"Nuisance!" Mills said. "The fact is, Gwen, my dear, I wanted to get a hint for my belated wedding present. What do you think Mrs. Walsh would like best?"

Gwendolyn meditated. "Every lady likes a nice bit of jewellery," she hazarded finally.

He shook his head. "I want to get something that she and Mr. Walsh can both use."

"What about something for the table?" she suggested. "Cut glass. You can never have too much cut glass. Much more genteel than silver, to my mind."

Mills said that he would look up Walsh himself and see if he could get his ideas on the subject.

"He might be at their house now being done up in Grosvenor Square," the parlourmaid suggested. "Just by chance, like. Or at one of his clubs."

"I'll try the house first. Might just catch them both there. Good idea, Gwennie!" And going farther into the hall, Mills promptly lifted down the telephone.

Walsh answered, and Mills asked if he might come along for a word or two.

"Certainly!" Arthur's tone was not pressing, but Mills jumped into his car and drove over at once.

Arthur met him civilly enough in the big drawing-room on the first floor, which looked very bare and smelled very much of fresh paint.

"I want to get some little trifle for a wedding present that will please both of you," Mills explained as they shook hands. "It was through me that you and Violet first met, really. I just missed her in Ennismore Gardens." He explained about his calling there for the same purpose.

Arthur said at once that he would prefer it to be something for Violet alone.

"Yes, but what?" Mills urged. Then he caught sight of a recess in which a hidden light lit up a large piece of Chinese plate.

"That's a pretty bit of colour," he said admiringly. He had a good eye for colour, and walked over to examine it closely.

Arthur kept step with him, glancing covertly at his watch as he did so. "When did the maid think Vi would be back?" he asked. But Mills only shook his head, and going up to the china cabinet he began to talk very knowledgeably of its exhibited contents. Mills knew a good deal about china. He knew a good deal about everything that you might possibly buy cheap and sell dear. Arthur's chill manner softened.

"Look at this bit," he said, taking a key from his pocket and unlocking the cabinet. "Here's a nice little piece that I found quite by chance." He held up the cup.

Mills was enthusiastic, but he did not take it in his hands. "I sometimes drop things," he explained with a half laugh. "But I don't think that it's Kang He, all the same. . . ."

Arthur did and they argued the pros and cons stubbornly. Each stuck to his own contention. Arthur had a book in the library that would settle the dispute, and he went down to the ground floor to fetch it. He found it and the passage he wanted and was just about to take the book up to Mills when the telephone rang shrilly. Mills also heard it and saw one instrument on the mantel beside him —not yet again hidden in its ornamental shell. It was evidently an extension of the one below in the library.

Mills lifted it off very quietly. He heard Arthur Walsh's voice saying: "This is No. 300 Grosvenor Square. Who's speaking?"

For a second there was no reply. Arthur thought he had been cut off, and was just about to replace the receiver when he heard a voice say urgently: "You are to gome at vunce to Stanley Mews. Mrs. Valsh says so. She has left the doors of the house and the flat unlocked. The segond-floor flat. She is there. Gome to her at vunce!" There was a click as of a receiver hung up.

Arthur stood waiting a moment, but nothing more came. "You've cut me off!" he said sharply in a tone of protesting and absolute bewilderment.

"What number, please?" asked a girl's voice. Evidently from the exchange.

"You've cut me off!" Arthur said furiously.

"Sorry. What number was it?"

Arthur had no idea. The instrument was dead. He hung up. The voice had had a strong German accent, or what we call German. It might have been Scandinavian or Danish or Czecho-Slovakian. The delivery had been rushing, and suggested a man tremendously excited, who had but a second in which to get his message understood. And the message itself . . .

He ran upstairs, and Arthur rarely ran. "Stanley Mews, isn't that where you are now living, Mills?"

Mills nodded.

"I've had a most extraordinary message from there, apparently from Vi!" Walsh repeated it.

"She must have gone there with her mother," Mills said carelessly. "Mrs. Finch has a key to my new digs. Well, are you off?"

"Just a moment." Arthur reached for the telephone. "What's its number?"

Mills gave it. "But you'll be there quicker than—" he began. Arthur silenced him by again asking for the number. Then he answered Mills.

"It wasn't Vi. It's some fool's idea of a hoax. I put one over on a chap at my club and he swore to get his own back. Can't get an answer." He turned questioningly to Mills. "Exchange says she can't get any reply. That proves it's a hoax. The chap was telephoning from my club, or his own home." Arthur hung up, and was turning away when the door opened and a servant entered to say that Miss Catherine Walsh was below in her car and would like a word with Mr. Walsh.

"I'm here myself," said a cordial voice behind the servant. "May I come in? The sun's too hot to exist in the street. Oh, Mr. Mills! How do you do?" Kitty appended frigidly. How excited the two men looked. Had they been quarrelling? She knew now that any critical touch on Violet would infallibly rouse Arthur to fury.

"Where's Vi, Arthur?" she asked her cousin. "I have a conciliatory message for her from Aunt Caroline that must be delivered at once. For aunt asks Vi to join her in her box at Covent Garden to-night. She's waiting impatiently for Vi's answer, and you know Aunt Caroline. Her invitation to be delivered ' instantly if not sooner.'" Kitty sighed. Dear Aunt Caroline was certainly fussy.

"Walsh has just had what purported to be an S.O.S. from Violet," Mills interrupted. "If so, she's now at my flat in an obscure but conveniently cheap place called Stanley Mews. It's over a garage owned by Mr. Gray. Well, Walsh, you'd better be off to my said humble digs, and find out whether the phone was a hoax or not."

"But what was the message?" Kitty asked.

"Oh, it was some idiot's idea of an exquisitely good hoax," Arthur said scornfully. "And the better to camouflage his identity he assumed a comical German accent; telling me that 'Mrs. Valsh' wanted me to come to her at Mills's flat 'at vunce,' before he prevented me from giving him my idea of a joke by hanging up, so that I couldn't ask another question."

"Vi might have got some one to telephone because she has had an accident," Kitty said uneasily, " as apparently Mrs. Finch was not with her to do it."

"Good God, what an awful thought!" Arthur jumped up from the chair into which he had flung himself. "I must get there instantly! Don't you come, Kitty," as she moved to go with him. "It's a hoax, I feel sure—one of Eastcastle's choicest. But still, your notion—Hurry, Mills, if you're coming as guide. That'll do me a good turn, as I don't know the place. My car's round the corner."

He kept his finger on the bell and ordered the man to bring his car round at once. "You cut along back to Aunt Caroline," he said kindly to his cousin; but Kitty utterly refused to be left behind for any minutes of doubt, and they all bundled into Arthur's waiting car. He stepped on the accelerator almost at once, too, with a pressure that belied his assurances to Kitty, and verbally to himself, that the phone-call could be nothing but a hoax.

"Yes, Chief Inspector Pointer speaking," said a calm voice at Scotland Yard in response to an agitated one coming through the telephone beside him. Seated at his office table though the speaker was, it could be seen that he was at least six feet in height, with a bronzed clean-shaven face that conveyed assurances of high intelligence and authority. The eyes were deep grey under finely drawn brows, dark brown like the lashes. The chin square, the lips looked equally capable of stern reserve or geniality. And when he presently moved and rose, his lean frame did so with the lithe unhurried swiftness of a powerful athlete at the acme of fitness. An unexpectedly young man, too, was this Chief Inspector Pointer; still, for all his professional renown, well under middle age. Unmistakably, even at a glance, a man of brains and formidable qualifications as a crime detective.

He listened intently, and then said quietly but with sharp conciseness: "Been dead some hours, you think. Of course you'll lock the door and guard it well from any intrusion whatsoever, or by any one, any one whomsoever until I get there. How about the window or windows? They look to the front, you say, and another constable is watching them and the entrance to the house. Good!"

Pointer hung up the phone, quickly but neatly tidied his papers, weighted them, rolled down the self-locking top of his writing-table, and went with long light steps down to a plain but notably efficient dark-green car standing ready for him in the inner courtyard of Scotland Yard.

The call had a quite special interest for him because the young woman reported murdered in a little flat in Stanley Mews was said to be the daughter of the notorious Mrs. Finch of the Little Owls night-clubs, about which such constant complaints used to reach the police.

There might be no connection, but it was odd that it should be her daughter . . . and that the owner of the flat where the body had been found was the stepfather of the dead woman.

The garage was run by a manager, a man called Cook, who bore a very good reputation indeed. As did Mr. Gray, for that matter. The manager was an ex-Service man who had risen to be a captain in the War but who sensibly called himself plain "Mister" nowadays. Cook was on the look-out for the Yard car. He stepped forward to the kerb at once and greeted Pointer warmly.

"Why on my premises, Mr. Pointer?" he asked plaintively. "Why not her own home? Or one of those gay and giddy clubs her mother used to run? The entrance is round the corner for the upper floors."

"Do they belong to your place too?" Pointer asked.

Cook nodded. "Three floors let to three gents. Luckily two are out at the moment. There's enough of a mob in there as it is. Girl's young husband, raving mad. Girl's best friend fainting in the corner; and it is a nasty sight, even for you, Chief Inspector. Tenant of the flat doing the splits all round to get the police—me—you—and all the world—here."

A second car had followed Pointer's and now drew up. Several men slipped out and waited. Cook, the garage manager, showed the way round the corner to a side door, out of sight from the garage itself, which was used by the occupiers of the upper floors.

On the doorstep stood Arthur Walsh, looking distraught.

"That's her husband," Cook whispered. "It's his wife that's murdered, and I thought we should need a strait-jacket."

Beside him was Ronald Mills. He, too, was white and shaken-looking. Pointer saw him turn and say something to a young girl dimly visible in the lobby behind him; for the front door was ajar.

Pointer was introduced by Cook, and Walsh said thickly: "Get the man who did it, superintendent, and you'll have a friend in me all my life!"

Mills said nothing except: "Shall I go up with you? They're my rooms. Unfortunately!"

"Can this young lady go home? It's been an awful shock for her," Cook asked Pointer in an aside. "It's a Miss Walsh—a cousin of his—" He nodded towards Arthur.

Pointer looked down into Kitty's face, as white as her organdie frock. The frock was as spotless as the snow-white elbow gloves. Not the frock for a murder, and not—by a long way—the face for a murderess either. Traits never seen in the face of a criminal were there: candour and sweetness and horrified pity. Violence of deed or word would be impossible to this young girl; though she now looked shattered by poignantly deep sympathy.

"I'll see her as soon as it's possible," Pointer assented gently. "Perhaps there's a room she can wait in?"

"There's my own room by the door, if you'll excuse its disorder," Cook said, opening it.

Kitty thanked them both with white lips and sat down by a table. There were two other doors in the passage. A back one leading into the garage, another one leading down the stairs to the kitchen offices.

"What are you delaying for?" Arthur Walsh demanded harshly, his face working. "She's up there! Murdered! My Violet! . . ."

"Shall I come up again?" Mills asked.

Pointer nodded, asked the manager to stop with Miss Walsh, and followed Mills up the stairs, Arthur hard on his heels. Four of the men from the Yard, who had come in the second car, followed them in a compact group.

The constable standing guard outside the locked door upstairs was sent down to help Cook keep a kindly but vigilant eye on Miss Walsh's shocked state.

Before stepping in through the front door of the flat, Pointer glanced up and down the narrow stairs. Its door was out of sight from the door above, or the door below. The linoleum that covered the landing looked neat and clean; no marks to suggest a crime appeared on it. The door into the flat was varnished and it, too, showed no marks on it. It opened directly into the sitting-room; a fairly large and quite comfortable room. This was the front room. The back room opening out of it had been divided into a small bedroom and a tiny bathroom. These made up the whole of the floor— and the flat.

In the front room before the fireplace lay the dead body of a young woman, apparently a lady. She was lying in the oddly shortened, crumpled-up way in which a body falls when it drops where it had been standing. The whole top of the head was a horrible sight. At least three terrific blows had been struck on it; any one of which must have caused instant death. On the mantel, almost over her head, was a modernist figure made from a flexible strip of steel with a steel head fastened to one end. The steel feet at the other end had been cast solidly in one with a thick square base of the same metal. Lifting it up with his gloves on, Pointer saw the red outline of the base on the marble. The green felt gummed to the base was a welter of blood.

One of his men tested it for fingerprints. It showed none. Then Pointer grasped it by the head and found what a terrible weapon it then became. The four metal corners of the inch-thick heavy steel base became so many steel axes. The flexible strip gave a powerful spring to the whole. A mere child could kill with it. But the child, Pointer reflected, would have had to know its fell weight. For it looked light, almost fragile.

Meantime Arthur Walsh had pushed roughly past Pointer and fallen unrestrainably down on his knees beneath the body. "Vi! Vi, my darling!" he agonisedly implored it, and would have turned the face up had not Pointer raised him, instead, to his feet.

"You'll only hinder us that way, sir," he said kindly but warningly. "Tell me in as few words as possible how this happened."

"But I haven't an idea," Arthur exclaimed with staring wild eyes. "In God's name tell me, inspector! What— has—happened?" he asked in choking tones of blank horror.

Pointer suggested that the distraught husband should go downstairs and wait for him there. Arthur Walsh stared at him, stared at the dreadful body of his young wife, and stumbled out of the room, Mills beside him.

On the hearth-rug just in front of the body were some torn-up scraps of paper. Pointer turned to his photographer: "I want a close-up of those papers too," he ordered, although as far as could be seen there was no writing on any of the bits.

While this was being done, Pointer stepped out on the landing and looked interrogatively at the constable, who saluted again and said rapidly:

"I was on my regular beat just round the corner from here, sir, at a quarter to six, all but, when the gentleman who's in the room behind you came rushing round the corner; and after him Mr. Cook, that I know quite well. The first one caught hold of my arm and gasped ' Murder!' And then Mr. Cook ran up and told me that a young lady had been brutally killed in one of the little flats over his garage. I turned to the entrance, and there was the gentleman who's just now stumbled down the stairs, and a young lady with him. They were beckoning madly to me from the top step. I looked at my watch and noted that it was just a quarter to six as I entered the front door, and followed the gentleman and the young lady who had been beckoning to me, and had waited for me on the top step. I found the body in there, quite dead and fairly cool to the touch. I didn't disturb it in any way, sir, of course; only touched the back of one of her hands. Then I blew my whistle gently, and when P.C. 2479 got here a minute later I sent him out to watch the house and immediately phoned to you, sir. A moment after that P.C. 9641 hurried up and I stationed him to watch the back of the premises."

CHAPTER SEVEN: CHIEF INSPECTOR POINTER GETS TO WORK

Pointer went on downstairs. He wanted to send Kitty home as soon as possible.

"Please tell me, Miss Walsh, just how you came to be here, and exactly what you found had happened here. I am very sorry to ask you for these facts, but I must. You gentlemen would wait outside," he added to the two men who had kept silently sympathetic company with her.

Alone with him, Kitty fixed on him a look of anguished horror as she answered faintly but bravely:

"I came thinking it might be a joke—the message, I mean, asking my cousin to come to her here at once . . . Mr. Mills was with him and we all three came, expecting my cousin, Arthur Walsh, as he quite believed, the intended victim of a stupid hoax or practical joke. My cousin suspected a booby trap, and went in first. But he gave an awful cry —a cry—"Kitty unconsciously put her hands again over her ears at its remembrance. Would she ever forget that cry of Arthur's, like the scream of a mortally stricken animal?

Pointer decided to ask her only one more question now. Since "we" meant the two others outside, presumably he could cover the ground without her help.

"You saw no one about, and heard no other sound in the flat?" he asked gently.

Kitty had not; and she was helped into a summoned taxi and driven back at once to her own people.

Then Pointer heard again, from its semi-dazed recipient himself, the bewildering phoned summons that finally—Arthur explained briefly—brought him incredulously to where the awful reality awaited him instead of the grotesque hoax he had intended to "properly pay off." And Pointer got him to write out for him the message exactly as it had sounded with its foreign pronunciation. As nearly as he could now time it, Arthur said, he had heard the last, suddenly cut-off word just before five-thirty.

Pointer let him off from further torture—as his questions visibly inflicted it—as soon as his duty could permit.

Cook, the garage manager, confirmed events. Mills had called him up on the house phone and he had found everything as already recited, and the murdered girl's half-crazed young husband fondling her shockingly struck-down form with wild caresses and appeals to his murdered wife to speak to him, look at him. It was an awful scene. The time, then, nearly quarter to six. He and Mills had forcibly dragged him away; telling Walsh he "must not move or touch" her before the police could see everything. At least Cook had; and Mills, on his urging, had helped him. "Besides," he added, "the barest glance made it only too sure that there was, could be, no spark of life in the poor thing."

Asking the husband to come in again, Pointer got from him a spate of distracted details. "Who phoned to me from here? Chief inspector, I shall go quite out of my mind unless you can tell me that. It's what I'd give my life to know! Was it the murderer I heard? Did he want to get at me by killing her? Was that why he told me I was wanted? Or did she need me, and had she really asked the speaker to give me that message . . . what I mean—" Walsh thrust out a hand that shook. "What I mean is, was some foreigner there? And had she really asked for that message to be sent me at once, and did the fool bungle it? Or was he by some means prevented from sending it until it was too late? The voice sounded as though he were in a frightful rush. I thought at the time, too —but, like the besotted fool that I was, thought it part of the hoax—that the speaker didn't want to be overheard, yet wanted to be very sure that I got the message all right."

Pointer's cool but not unkindly eyes took stock of the emotion-swept face before him. Yes, the young man was making strenuous efforts to be precise, he thought; was seeking to put into words the feelings roused by that strange, and under the circumstances, dreadful appeal; made apparently on behalf of his murdered young wife. And made in vain.

"Would it have saved her, do you think, if I had gone immediately—got here at once?" Arthur asked in agonised tones.

Pointer could not say. He was sorry for the terrible tension in those questions.

"Had you ever heard the voice before, do you think?" he asked.

"Never, so far as I know. And yet, somehow, there's a beastly feeling that I ought to have," Arthur muttered thickly.

"Just what do you mean?" Pointer asked with interest.

Walsh made a sort of swimming motion with his out-thrown hands. "I don't know," he said wearily. "It's just that. Just a vague impression that I really ought to know that voice. But I can't express it. It's just a feeling . . . and I wasn't conscious even of that until you asked me."

"And you, Mr. Mills?" Pointer turned now to the man who, with a very wooden face, stood a little behind the other. "What time did you leave your flat?"

"I left here on Friday last. I've been staying down at Maidenhead with Mrs. Finch—that's Mrs. Walsh's mother—I'm her partner more or less, unfortunately, in those Little Owls clubs of hers that have gone bust. She needed some papers she had left in her house in Ennismore Gardens. I rushed up for them and got to her house about quarter-past five. The parlourmaid thought Mrs. Walsh was in. Said she had just heard her in her bedroom. But she must have just gone out, the maid came back to tell me."

"If Mrs. Walsh was seen at a quarter-past five by the parlourmaid, it's very important," Pointer said slowly.

"A bit after the quarter-past possibly," Mills said on thinking back. "But I didn't really notice the time. I had intended, besides getting the papers, to find out what she would like as a belated wedding present. I thought she might be at Grosvenor Square. Or, if not, that Walsh might be there; so I phoned there, found that he was, and went round. And while I was talking to him Walsh received that mysterious message over his house phone.

"Miss Kitty Walsh also happened in just then, for a word with Mrs. Walsh, and we all three came along together. We found the door unlocked as the message had said—and found Mrs. Walsh dead! As the message had certainly not said. Look here, chief inspector, they've told me over the phone that Mrs. Finch has left the solicitor's office at Maidenhead; but even so I think I can find her. I know where she's likely to go and where not. . . . Have you any objections if I rush off for her in my car?"

In reply to further questions Mills said he had given up his clubs for economy's sake; but he would go to the Westmorland Hotel for the time being, supposing he could get a room there. Anyhow he would ring up and let Pointer know where he could be found, since his flat was in the hands of the police.

"Thank you, sir. But now before you go, will you take a very careful look over your flat and let me know if anything is missing, so far as you can detect; or if anything has had its position shifted since you noticed it last. Or if anything has been added? I want you carefully to observe these points; but without touching things at all."

Pointer walked through the rooms with Mills, who said in a moment that the little steel figure had been standing in the centre of the mantel as usual, when he last saw it. It did not belong to him. It was in the flat when he took it furnished. A few things of his own had been added; but, as he said, not that horribly used steel article.

Mills was allowed to drive off after that. Pointer noticed that he took a curt farewell of Walsh, who apparently did not hear it as he stood staring straight before him with a set rigid look on his face.

The doctor had not yet arrived, so Pointer had Cook also go over the flat with him, to see if anything was noticeably altered in it. Cook could not be certain, as he did not go much into the rooms. But as far as he could say, the only striking difference was "in respect of the ornamental steel figure, which had played so dreadful a part in the tragedy."

For he had himself placed it on the very middle of the mantelshelf. And when he had chanced to be in the sitting-room of the flat for a moment on Thursday last he had seen it still where he had put it. The figure was all steel; and Mr. Gray, who owned it, had told him that it represented the "Genius of Machinery." Gray valued it but—although it looked so light and fragile—it was really so heavy, and so awkward to handle, that Gray, who used to have it in his office downstairs, had wished it to be kept in the furnished flat let off above.

"Was Mr. Gray often there?" Pointer asked.

"Not much, just now," was the reply. "His works are at Hendon, where he is busy with a new engine that he is putting on the market shortly." Cook then went on to speak of the tenants in the house. The first floor was let to a doctor who had had it for three years. Cook gave him a very good reputation: quiet, studious, giving no trouble whatever. The second floor had been let about six months ago to the Mr. Ronald Mills who just left. Mills had come there from a very smart suite house by the Park. "He seems right enough," continued Cook, "but he's mixed up in the Little Owls night-clubs; so you never know." The top floor was let to an elderly newspaper man who was "away on some journalism stunt nine-tenths of the time, and is away on one now, I fancy. He, too, is a permanent tenant," added the garage manager, "and a thoroughly good sort; a reliable steady chap." As to front door, each tenant had a latch-key, of course. "Mr. Gray? Oh, probably, yes. He may still have his old one; but he has no use for it, if so. He only comes occasionally for a word of business about the garage, or some repairs to the house. And in that last case he just pops up to see what is wanted, and we go over the accounts afterwards."

Cook was needed in the garage at this moment; and the doctor now came in. He had been delayed by a street accident. At sight of the horribly battered head he frowned as he bent over it. "Hatred here, surely," he ejaculated. "The first blow killed her. The two others were sheer fury, or nerves." His eye followed Pointer's to the steel object that had done it.

"May I lift the thing?" he asked.

Pointer assented. He said that it had been thoroughly tested for fingerprints, but none had been anywhere on it.

Gloves on, Doctor Ward-Bentley lifted the figure, held it by the head and whipped it through the air, looking meaningly at Pointer and then at the green baize on the bottom of its stand.

"That's the weapon, eh? And a more deadly little springboard I never handled. One tap"—he gestured to the crushed-in head of the victim. "Given this, those successive blows may have been sheer ignorance. I mean that the murderer may have had no conception of the result that would follow one blow, and so have struck those savagely unnecessary blows to make sure that she could never speak."

He agreed with the chief inspector that the dead young woman had been standing—probably smoking a cigarette since one lay just beyond her hand— and had been struck down from the side. In other words, some one had come up beside her, snatched up the steel figure on the mantel, and suddenly brought it down with full force on her head. The murderer had either been taller than the young woman, or she had been bending slightly down for something. As to when she had been killed, the doctor could only say that it was at least an hour ago and he would not be surprised to learn that it was two hours ago, now. But not more, he thought.

There was a knock on the door.

"Gentleman asks to see you, sir—"the constable began, "and begs for a word with Chief Inspector Pointer if he will forgive the intrusion at Mr. Walsh's request." The said gentleman being one Sewell, by name: "Victor Sewell, to be quite explicit," said a pleasant voice over the constable's shoulder before the owner of the voice came forward to meet Pointer's outstretched hand in a cordial clasp.

For Pointer knew the young man quite well, and had no little esteem for both his personal and his professional character; more particularly since his brilliantly successful clearing of a great name from undeserved calumny.

"Walsh is outside," the caller said in a low tone. "Mayn't he come in? I think it might be a boon to him if he thought that he was helping you on to the murderer's trail. He only married the poor girl a week ago." Pointer had no objection whatever. The other way round. It had been only for Walsh's own sake that—for the moment—he had left him on one side as much as possible. Sewell explained how he himself had been professionally brought into the case; how, immediately the police had been summoned, Walsh had got Cook to phone for Sewell also.

On being shown the murdered young wife of his friend, the Private Investigator was profoundly shocked. For, as he told Pointer, she had been his charming hostess at lunch only a couple of hours before. His sympathy was, therefore, deeper even than Pointer's when, on being allowed in again, Arthur chokingly asked to be left alone with his dead bride until the stretcher-bearers came to take her away.

But Violet Walsh's remains belonged now to the investigations of Scotland Yard. And her unhappy husband had to be told that a constable must remain in the room. With this necessary proviso, however, Arthur was left alone with his dead until the stretcher arrived. And meantime Sewell went into fuller details of the mysteriously exchanged pearl necklace, repeating to Pointer all that poor Violet had herself dilated on at luncheon.

"She told you she always wore the longer string?" Pointer said. "She hasn't it on here. She is wearing no necklace, as you see."

"Might she have dropped the string into her handbag?" queried Sewell.

"She seems to have no handbag, or what advertisements call a 'pochette,' along with her. That looks as though she had come in a car where she might have left it. Her shoes suggest a car, too. It's a very dusty day and they are quite fresh-looking. She has apparently not worn gloves, either. But I haven't had a thorough search made yet."

At this moment the bearers arrived with the stretcher and Violet Walsh's body was borne away. Simultaneously with the closing of the house door behind it Arthur seemed—with a shuddering deep breath—to resolutely shut the door of his will upon his private emotions, as he turned to Sewell, saying: "For God's sake, give me some active work to do, if it's only fetching and carrying on the trail of her murderer! There must be some link between those exchanged pearls and her death!"

He made a sweeping gesture and wheeled to face the chief inspector. Their eyes met, and Pointer wondered if the same suspicion that was coursing among others in his own brain had suddenly entered Walsh's, as the latter exclaimed: "Our talk at luncheon must have made Vi think of something—recall something—connected with these rooms. She came here to discover something! Who was here? Who let her in? Who phoned that message to me? I've a ghastly notion, chief inspector, that it was the very man that killed her! But if so why?—why . . .?"

He dropped heavily into a chair and covered his wild eyes with his hands. After a moment's silence Pointer asked him if Mrs. Walsh usually carried a purse or handkerchief bag. "Always," was Arthur's instant reply. "She never went out of the house without it. Why do you ask?"

"Because," Pointer answered, "no such article has yet been found in the room. If she had one with her it has either been removed or very effectively hidden up to now."

He had already had the bloodstained hearth-rug taken away. The papers that had been lying around Violet's body had also been collected by one of his men and now lay on the table as they had been photographed. They were all blank, but Pointer, too, only handled them with rubber gloves on.

Walsh shook his head when asked if he had seen any papers like them. Staying as they were in Mrs. Finch's house until their own could be redecorated —he never called Violet's mother anything but "Mrs. Finch "—he could not say. But he stared at the blank white fragments in perplexity.

Pointer soon after discovered the missing little handbag—stuffed far down at the back of the seat of an upholstered arm-chair. So far down, thrust so deeply, that it might easily have failed altogether to be found.

"Vi never did that!" Arthur exclaimed sharply, as he saw the inspector dig it out.

Sewell and Pointer were not so sure—as a glance which the former shot at the impassive Scotland Yard man said. Mrs. Walsh might have felt herself in danger . . . might have hidden there some valuable clue. . . . Sewell's heart beat faster at the thought.

Pointer carefully emptied the little bag on to a sheet of paper and Sewell jotted down the items. A gold vanity case with powder "compact"— rouge, lipstick, and eyebrow pencil—in it. A purse with some change in it and a couple of pound notes . . . a handkerchief. That was all.

Arthur stared at it with straining eyes. "Her bag . . .! We bought it together . . .! It's a nightmare."

"Look here, Walsh," Sewell urged insistently. "Go down to your house in the country. You can't help—really. And it's only tearing your heart afresh for nothing. We'll ring you up—or I'll dash down there—the first moment you can be of any use. What do you say, chief inspector?"

"I think it a good idea. Is Colonel Walsh in the country?"

"He's up in Town," Arthur said indifferently.

"At his Club?" Pointer pressed. "We would like to spare you from having to break the news," he explained in compassionate tones.

"Probably," was all Arthur knew as to that last question.

Pointer just glanced at Sewell, who went to the telephone in the lobby—to try the In and Out for Colonel Walsh.

"I won't detain you but a moment longer, Mr. Walsh," Pointer added, " but I must ask you about Mrs. Walsh's plans for the afternoon."

Arthur said that she had spoken at lunch of an afternoon with her dressmaker. She intended to fit herself out completely: country frocks, town afternoon frocks, evening things. She meant to be thorough, she had said, so as to be quite free afterwards. He gave the name of the House in question. Pointer knew it as an establishment where a woman could easily while away a whole day, let alone an afternoon. Arthur said that she had intended to drop in at Grosvenor Square as soon as she got free, as they were doing up the large drawing-room and some of the bedrooms, and she particularly wanted to see the effect of the tints that she had chosen. He himself had driven his wife to Bruton Street, and then gone on to Grosvenor Square. That would have been about three o'clock, he thought. He had had a good many letters to answer, and sat writing and glancing through estimates for new wine vaults until Mills was shown in at a little before half-past five. Mills said he would wait for Mrs. Walsh if he wasn't in the way. "We talked about—"Arthur said

vaguely.

"About—" Pointer questioned as to the subject.

For a moment Arthur could not remember, then it came to him:

"Some china I had in a cabinet. I looked up a book on Chinese Ceramics to prove a point, and was reading it when the telephone rang. I felt sure it was from my wife, glanced at the clock, and picked up the instrument." He repeated that to the best of his belief the time had been just before the half-hour. Mills, he thought, had been with him only three or four minutes then. He went again over his certainty that it was Lord Eastcastle's idea of a joke, the arrival of his cousin, and her startling suggestion that the message might have been genuine, their drive to the Mews—and— Here he stopped dead.

Pointer thanked him, endorsed the suggestion that he go down to their place in the country, and with Sewell's help finally got him into his car. One of Pointer's men got in beside Arthur and took the wheel—for he was obviously in no state to drive even a perambulator, they all agreed.

But he would, of course, be "shadowed" everywhere and unremittingly until Scotland Yard's problem—who murdered Violet Walsh?—should be effectively solved. Nothing and no one could prevent that. The kindly probabilities were, how-

ever, that Arthur himself would remain unconscious of any "shadow" other than that of his own obsessing concern.

"By the way, Mr. Walsh," Pointer paused in shutting the door of the car to add, "can you remember if by chance Mr. Mills had his gloves on if he handled anything from your Chinese cabinet when you and he were discussing its contents. We have to list all fingerprints connected in any way with the case, you know; and if Mr. Mills left his on a piece of china it would save us troubling him for another print."

"I seem to recall that he kept his left glove on. But I don't remember if he handled any piece," Arthur said with a visible effort to recall the scene. His face suddenly flushed, and he leaned forward as if to say something else, or ask some eager question. Then his previous look of absolutely exhausted emotion and consequent blank apathy swept over it again, and he closed his eyes wearily as he leaned back. The man at the wheel, at a slight indication from Pointer as he firmly shut the door, started up the car, which at once sped its forlorn-looking occupant out of sight.

"I thought you were getting Mills' fingerprints when you handed him your sketch of his rooms and got him to initial it as correct," Sewell remarked with an inquiring look at the chief inspector.

"I was," Pointer agreed dryly.

"So you simply wanted, just now, to learn about his gloves? Useful detail! Especially as I noticed their absence."

"Yes, he had slipped them inside his waistcoat, I saw," Pointer said with one of his characteristically undecipherable smiles.

Sewell shot a silent glance at him, but Pointer was studying his shoe tips until he looked up to ask if Sewell had located Colonel Walsh. Sewell had not. The Colonel had lunched at the Army and Navy alone, but left there. And its hall-porter could only say that Colonel Walsh had not reserved a room there for the night.

CHAPTER EIGHT: A KEY-RING IS MISSED

Pointer picked up his hat and, after a word with the sergeant whom he left in charge, made a move towards his own car.

"Where to?" Sewell asked. "I'm Mary's little lamb, you know."

"I must try for the whereabouts of the necklace. Did you notice the absence from the murdered woman's handbag of an item that one would have quite expected to find in it?"

Sewell shook his head. "No, I missed nothing—and so evidently I missed something important. What was it?'"

"Her keys," Pointer replied. "Yet the very valuable larger pearl necklace isn't on her, nor with her. The keys may have been taken out when her handbag was forced down out of sight and almost out of touch in that chair."

"I don't see why you're so sure that she herself didn't thrust it there," Sewell said. At least some half-dozen good reasons why Mrs. Walsh might well have done so were in his own mind.

"There are a few small drops of dried blood on one side of the bag," Pointer said, "as though it had been lying not far from her when she was struck down. The drops had dried where they lighted, which suggests that either the murderer overlooked their evidence or trusted that it would not be discovered, or hoped to regain the bag when he could safely destroy it."

Sewell drew a long breath. He had never worked on a capital charge before. In a sense he was not doing so here. For his sole province was the clearing of Violet Walsh's reputation from the charge of her having criminally raised money on a necklace which she knew to be fraudulent.

"You know," Sewell said as he lighted a fresh cigarette, "going by faces, I should expect young Mrs. Walsh to have always locked her jewels up with extreme care."

Pointer cocked an inquiring eye at him as he, too, lit up.

"I lunched with her—them—you know. And—well, I should expect her to look sharply after her possessions. It was indicated in her face. Her mouth, for instance—"

"Looked locked-up, too?" Pointer suggested with a twinkle.

Sewell nodded. "It did! 'Secretive,' I tabulated her. But with such high spirits and 'go' that I could quite see how a rather cold fish like Walsh would be seized by the—the—" He groped for the right word to exactly express his meaning.

"Gulf Stream?" Pointer tentatively supplied. And Sewell nodded his thanks for its fitness.

"—Of her temperament," he went on. "The zest of her honeymoon was vivid in Walsh's gay young bride, then. And now she's dust and ashes; or will be in a short time!" Sewell was evidently deeply moved by the sudden tragedy into which he had been personally drawn.

"Was that her usual manner, I wonder?" Pointer queried aloud. Or was she keyed up about something . . . expecting something—good or ill?"

"I'm handicapped by never having met her before. But if she was just as usual, she was certainly dashed amusing company," Sewell said. "Not witty, let alone brilliant. Nothing of that mentality. Just chock full of high spirits. She laughed contagiously at the smallest jest."

A constable came up to Pointer as the two were getting into the Yard car. "There's a gentleman here, sir, name of Walsh, too, just stepped into the garage. Wears a clergyman's collar and asks for a word with yourself."

Pointer went round to the garage door at once. Ambrose Walsh—Father Walsh—was there. Pointer, who had not before met him, was struck by the intense pallor of his face and his air of aloofness.

"I happened to be in one of the houses opposite," began Ambrose in his charming voice, "teaching a little blind boy his religious lessons." He handed his card to Pointer. "And when I came out just now and asked the reason for the crowd over here I was variously informed that there had been 'a death,' 'a murder,' 'a suicide. . . .' The name attached to each of these versions was ' Mrs. Walsh.' Now, there is a Mrs. Walsh who is a connection of mine by marriage. . . ." He looked inquiringly at Pointer.

"Mrs. Arthur Walsh is the lady's name, sir," Pointer said. And Father Ambrose was tensely silent for a full minute before he said quietly, "That is the name of my family connection. Is her husband here by any chance?"

Pointer explained a little, a very restricted little, of the tragedy. Ambrose listened with the close attention to be expected, while his pallor grew still more noticeable.

"Did you know the murdered lady well—may I ask, sir?" Pointer asked.

"I met her once. Before her marriage," was the reply. "Have you any theory, chief inspector, as to the motive for the crime? Or is it out of order to ask that question yet, if at all?"

Pointer looked at the speaker attentively. He appreciated the force of the personality confronting him. But besides that—as he looked into the dark resolute eyes on a level with his own, and he himself was well over six feet—he was conscious of a curious sensation as though a thick wall of ice or crystal were between himself and the priest. Something that neither he nor any man could pass through, except by the will of the other.

"May I ask exactly where you were visiting, sir, when you saw the crowd?" he asked instead of replying.

"Around the corner here is another garage, on the opposite side of the street. Over it are some tenements. I was in a room of which the window looks into a courtyard. So that I had no idea of this crowd—until I found it blocking my path."

"You know Mr. Sewell perhaps, sir?" Pointer turned towards his companion as he asked.

The priest's eyes seemed to grow hooded as he slowly said that he did, apologising formally for not having previously noticed Sewell, with whom he shook hands.

"Do you also know about the matter that Walsh has asked me to clear up?" Sewell asked.

"Yes," Ambrose said rather curtly. "Arthur told me that he was getting you to help him solve a mystery. Which would now appear to be entangled in a darker mystery," he murmured in a voice that suggested that his thoughts were elsewhere. "Strange . . .!"

"What is?" Sewell prodded.

"Strange that I should happen to be just across the road."

It is said that love cannot be hidden. And Pointer would have supplemented that axiom by another certitude, namely, that knowledge is equally bound to betray itself. And that the priest had some private knowledge pertinent to the murder of Violet Walsh, he felt certain. Of the extent or importance of that very deliberately unavowed knowledge, Pointer could as yet form no opinion. But he felt convinced that to Father Walsh himself it bulked weightily. Which made Pointer force the issue by asking with stern gravity: "Do you know anything, sir, bearing at all on the facts of the crime or charges now under police investigation?"

The priest's eyes met his as if all .the blinds were down in a house, as he said concisely: "No." Upon which monosyllabic negative, Ambrose Walsh walked unhindered away, after a stiff farewell nod to the two men. Unhindered, because Pointer considered the whereabouts of the larger pearl necklace more important than endeavouring to get through or over the barrier with which the priestly mind was hedged around at present.

As Sewell and he got into Pointer's car and left the spot the latter looked questioningly at his companion.

"You want me, I see, to pay for my official keep," laughed Sewell. "About Father Walsh, for instance. Well, I really know little of any consequence about him. He's distinctly out of my usual line of business. He's considered, I hear, to be marked for something high in the priesthood. But I'm inclined to think a mischievous agent here, he's so bigoted. I have a friend, the doctor for a couple of Convents, and, like myself, a Catholic, from whom I gather that Father Walsh practically forbids them taking in any Protestant children. They are jolly expensive convents, so it isn't any case of cruel discrimination. But it's Father Walsh's idee fixe that the true believer and the false believer, or heretic, should be kept apart, for fear of the rot spreading. I noticed, and so of course you had, chief inspector"—Sewell gave Pointer a friendly smile—"that he didn't refer to the murder as a 'terrible' or even a 'tragic' affair. And I can only wonder if he sees in it something grotesquely like 'divine providence.' He fairly raved against the marriage, Arthur Walsh told me, when going into the pearl mystery with me."

"How did he learn of the trouble about the pearls?" Pointer asked.

"Oh, the Walshes are good Catholics. So, too, is Ann Lovelace. Probably they all go to him to confession, when he's available."

"Could he tell us about knowing of it, if he had learnt of it only in that way?" Pointer asked, though he knew the answer.

"No, evidently Miss Lovelace or Arthur Walsh went to him about it as to a friend. Anyway, Arthur Walsh told me that his cousin, Father Ambrose Walsh, knew and was fanatically against the marriage. The Walshes are rather big fish with us. Their money, and the fact that they were pre-reformation Catholics. ... A totally different set, socially, from that of Violet Finch."

"Her father was a barrister, though, wasn't he?" Pointer asked. He knew all about the Finches from the Yard's information; but he might get some fresh news from Sewell's angle.

"Yes. Dublin. Mrs. Finch is a doctor's daughter. They were bitterly poor, she says, when her first husband died, leaving her with about seven hundred pounds in all and a baby girl, Violet Finch, to provide for. Mrs. Finch put most of the money into the management of a Social Club, to which she went herself. According to her—and I fancy her boasting is founded on fact—she doubled its membership in a month and trebled it in a quarter. She then sold her share for twice what she had put in, and started a night-club herself in a London cellar. It became the first of her gold mines, those Little Owls—"

"About which the Yard had daily complaints," Pointer interrupted with a grim smile. "But we know of no reason why they have quite faded out of late."

"Just fashion!" Sewell said sagely. "Got too popular to be popular any longer. Her prices, too, were fantastic. It was only while it was 'the thing' to be seen there that she could get them. Yet once she put them down, the end was in sight. Personally, I'm glad of it. If half the things I've heard about her and her clubs are true, they've ruined many a young fool between them. The gambling that went on there was incredible."

"How was it, may I ask, that you never happened to meet her daughter, Mrs. Walsh, until at to-day's lunch?"

"Her mother, it seems, wouldn't allow Miss Violet Finch to go to the Clubs. At least not until the fateful night when she and Walsh met. He told me that it was a case of love at first sight. And real love, too, it must have been, or he wouldn't have married into that lot. Though I have an idea that he didn't learn just who she was until they were mutually infatuated. I suppose she took after her father. Miss Kitty Walsh, I know, liked her. And that's a very good recommendation indeed to my thinking."

"Did Mrs. Walsh strike you as straightforward?" Pointer asked next.

"Rather! No finesse, and not much tact, probably. But I should think she'd be outspoken to a fault. 'Steel-true, blade straight, The great artificer Made my mate '—that sort. Poor Walsh! I wonder what the enigma of those changed pearls will prove to be. You know, chief inspector— Walsh's idea that his wife was hot on the right track strikes me as quite possible. She was distinctly the kind that—if she had come on something or thought of something vital—would have gone straight to have it out, face to face!"

There was a pause. Sewell's monkey brow worked furiously. "I suppose you know all about that chap Mills?" he burst out finally.

"No," Pointer replied promptly. "Not necessarily 'all,' but a good deal. He's not yet been found doing anything—"

"Apprehensible," finished Sewell with a grin.

"Precisely," Pointer agreed. "You always did get the right word, I remember."

"And you the right man! I'm jolly glad of a chance to work with you. I may have my own theories as we go along, but I won't expound them until the end of this case. Then I'll own up handsomely. And it isn't as if you needed any help from me. Nor, for that matter, do you ever parade what you're after till you've pretty well got your hand on it—my dear Pointer. But—to return to our mutton—Mills is a Cambridge man, with some quite decent family connections—for whatever these details may seem worth, though I expect they're all already in your bag."

Nothing more was said at the moment until Sewell, as usual, said it by asking: "What do you think oddest in what we've been told, so far, in this most extraordinary case, chief inspector?"

"That telephone message to the husband," Pointer unhesitatingly answered. And Sewell nodded his

complete agreement before—as usual—expanding the
problem with perhaps its most salient mystery: "What
could have been its motive? Personally, I can't account for
it by any conceivable reason for it."

"It's just possible that it was from some one who
wanted to make quite sure that Mr. Walsh would not be
in his mother-in-law's house at a given hour," Pointer
said. "There are many other possibilities, of course, but
that suggests itself as the simplest explanation. Which
was why I looked for her keys at once."

"And they're missing!" Sewell's forehead began to
corrugate portentously. And when Pointer added, "Yes,
it's possible that the murderer then hurried after the
much-more-valuable string of pearls, if he found to his
disappointment that his victim did not have it on," Sewell
said with emphasis, "Five thousand pounds, at least, in
question! And Walsh was told, when he bought the two,
that this string alone might easily fetch another
thousand."

"Then why didn't the vendor wait for such an
occasion? Who sold them? Do you know?" Pointer asked.

"The two necklaces belonged to old Lady Loudwater.
Oddly enough I chanced to hear, some months ago, that
she wanted to realise on them. They once belonged to
Queen Charlotte of Mexico and Lady Loudwater believed
they brought their owner bad luck. She rather suspected
that that was why they had been sold to her originally. If
so, they have assuredly lived up to their reputation!"

There followed another ruminating silence before
Pointer asked:

"Do you know Miss Lovelace?"

Sewell had often met her. "It was thought at one time
that she was going to marry Lord Wilverstone—or,
rather, that he would break off his engagement to
another girl and marry Ann Lovelace. But he married
t'other girl after all; so probably there was nothing in the
chatter. At that time Walsh, I know, was completely
bowled over by her. But she never even spared him an

encouraging glance. So that, too, evidently, melted away. Certainly he was head over ears in love with his wife, as I can testify, both from what he said to me when asking me to clear up the mystery of the false pearls and from my own observations at lunch to-day."

"Did she seem to you equally in love with him?" Pointer asked.

"Equally? No!" Sewell replied. "His evident adoration would have been hard to equal. But in love all the same. I mean that I think she was much more of the femme maitresse than he was of the homme maitre. Dear me!" he grinned, "I'm not as a rule addicted to French chestnuts; but one must borrow such phrases, at times, to get one's exact meaning defined without too much verbiage."

CHAPTER NINE: POINTER FINDS THE MISSING KEYS

Just before the car stopped, Pointer explained the police position:

"To a certain extent I have no right to enter the house. But if I had asked permission to do so, it would of course have been granted at once by Mr. Walsh. And I want, if possible, to have a look around Mrs. Walsh's own room, without the servants knowing that I have been in. Apparently no one has yet informed them of the murder. I have brought some keys with me, one of which ought to open the front door. If we're detected, I shall hide behind you. They know you lunched there, and I shall say that Mr. Walsh handed you his key and asked you to be kind enough to get something he forgot—"

"His umbrella," suggested Sewell ironically.

They got out of the car very quietly. Pointer tried a key with which, with a little manipulation, he silently opened the front door.

"Methods of the Yard," murmured Sewell, stepping in after him. His grin faded, though, as he softly shut the door behind him.

He had stood in this hall only a few hours ago; and now the murdered body of the laughing girl who had waved adieu to him from that very door was lying in a mortuary waiting for the dissection that must come.

"Have you any idea where her bedroom would be?" Pointer had asked on the way there. And Sewell had remembered her speaking of the noise of some adjacent flats that were being built, but the noise of which, "fortunately," they did not hear, because their bedroom was "at the back —overlooking the gardens."

The muffled sound of a wireless in the basement reached them from below, and the two hurriedly but very quietly slipped upstairs and found the desired room almost at once. It was a big room, over-sumptuously furnished with rose-satin frills decorating dressing-table, bedspreads, and windows. The furniture was old and good, and yet it looked over ornate. Three large wardrobe-trunks stood on the carpet. They were marked "V. W." Two smaller ones, marked " A. W." stood in the adjoining dressing-room.

Pointer shut and locked the doors of both rooms, and then walked slowly through them, eyeing the furniture and pulling on a pair of rubber gloves after handing another pair to Sewell. He lifted one or two things up from table or narrow mantel. But the wanted keys were not under them. Presently, however, his inspection reached the dressing-table with swinging mirror above it and little drawers at its sides. These latter were all locked, but one which had not been shut in as tightly as the others, and its corners projected a fraction of an inch. Inside were some dainty net and lace ruffles, and, quite at the back, on top of their fluffy froth, lay a small bunch of keys.

On testing the drawer for fingerprints, with a compact little pocket apparatus which he always had with him when on official duty, Pointer found —on parts where the surface had taken them— distinctly marked prints of three fingertips. The first one a rather pointed finger, the second and third decidedly square. They were very near the corner, and very much on the slant. It looked to Pointer as though the drawer had been closed in a great hurry by some one hurrying off.

They were not left by Mrs. Walsh's fingers—of that he felt quite positive. She had a rather large hand, with a very pointed third finger; and the nails of all her fingers were much longer than the nails on the hand in question. For these fingertips had had short nails. Pointer thought that these prints betokened the hand of a man. With the tiny camera which likewise accompanied him on such investigation Pointer photographed the marks carefully.

Sewell was keenly interested in all this. "Finger-prints are beyond me," he confessed. "Nothing amuses me more in detective stories than when an amateur gives one glance at a fingerprint and instantly identifies it. Whereas all such prints seem much of a muchness to me."

The chief inspector, however, could distinguish fingerprints well and he felt sure that he knew these. At the Yard, moreover, were experts who would read them as easily as other people read ordinary print. With which reinforcing thought Pointer again opened the drawer, and once more studied the keys closely without touching them in the first instance.

He thought they had been tossed in by some one in desperate haste. And he very much doubted whether Violet Walsh would have ever flung them on top of those pretty furbelows which seemed to have been laid in with care; and which, as he finally lifted out the comparatively heavy bunch of keys, showed too many signs of crushing to be worn again without first being redressed.

The keys themselves, when examined, told but little. Passing to the three wardrobe-trunks, he unlocked each in turn, and glanced through its contents. All were packed to overflowing, and very neatly and efficiently packed, too. Violet Walsh had been used to packing for herself. Finally he bent over a flat cabin trunk that had been shoved under one of the beds. A bed in the corner, which Pointer fancied—rightly, from the tapestry panels around it—had been Violet's before her marriage. When he unlocked this trunk and looked inside it he glanced round at Sewell, who was at his side in an instant.

"Something's been removed from this tray. Look!" He showed where, among a closely-stocked welter of jumpers, there was an empty space which exposed the bottom of the tray for nearly a quarter of its entire length.

"Seems to indicate that a box had occupied that empty space," Pointer said. "Such a box might have been a shallow, locked dispatch box that would guard papers or trinkets. Say—"

"A pearl necklace," Sewell interpolated with conviction as Pointer continued to study the tray, lifted it, glanced at the closely-packed lower part —untouched, he thought—before he re-locked this cabin trunk and shoved it back where he had found it.

The edge of the pink satin frilling around the bedspread was torn in one place. Pointer thought it had caught in the lock of the trunk and been violently pulled free.

"It certainly looks to me," said Sewell, "as though the larger pearl necklace was at the bottom of the murder— and of the telephone message summoning Walsh to the Mews so as to leave his wife's rooms free for the murderous brute to ransack in security for her jewels."

"You think her murderer wouldn't have seen that she wasn't wearing the pearls?" Pointer asked sceptically. "They certainly stand for at least one possible motive; and, so far, the only plausible one yet found. But why was she at the Mews at all? How did she get in? With her mother's key—Mr. Mills suggests. But, even so, that explains nothing as to her presence there at all—even apart from her murder. Why was she there?"

"Oh, it must have been connected with the lost or fraudulently exchanged string!" Sewell said. "She didn't look one to run after false gods. And it would surely have been a bit early for that, anyhow, the first week of her honeymoon!"

"Why wouldn't you have thought her the kind to have a love affair—with any one but her husband, I suppose you mean." Even without the curious affair of the pearls, Mrs. Walsh's character was highly important. Sewell considered. He was as keen as Pointer himself at "sensing" character. He even liked to consider himself unusually psychic. But the difficulty was how to put "feelings" into words without giving them the lie. "Well— she seemed to lack romantic tendencies. ... In a way, she lacked charm," he said finally. "One didn't notice it at first, you know, because she was so gay and breezy and even bluff. But, now you ask me, I don't think she was a lover by nature."

Sewell was interested in his own words. Like a man seeing a cloudy mixture settle to a different colour sediment, he regarded this decanted summary of Violet Walsh as something quite different from his vague general notions of bright eyes, red lips and gleaming teeth.

"Not much heart?" Pointer said. "Even her dead face suggests something of that sort. It's handsome—but, for her age, hard—very hard in what must have been its natural cast."

"Yes, perhaps she was inwardly hard. I told you Walsh adored her, rather than she him. You felt with him that she was the only thing in the world that mattered. Whereas "—Sewell saw the sediment clearing a little—" I fancy money and position and, above all, power, might appeal more to her. But look here, chief inspector, your questions are rather rummy. . . . I've noticed it before. They make you think of people differently. . . . Or, rather, they make you realise that you really thought of people differently from what you thought you did."

"It's the Scotland Yard touch," chaffed Pointer. "They teach us to strip off the glamour—"

"Ah!" Sewell put up a brown, bony hand impressively. "That's it! Just what she lacked. As I read Arthur Walsh's bride, she was without any touch of glamour. . . . But to go back to the question of motive for her murder—I don't see that the murderer mightn't have thought she was wearing that valuable string under her dress. Women often do, I've understood, when going about in ordinary street things."

"Sounds a bit hasty," Pointer said dryly, "to murder on an off-chance. And murderers, in my experience, are devilish careful, as a rule, not to put their necks into the noose for nothing. This one, too, had only to use his eyes.

For his victim is wearing a collarless, V-necked dress. And—unless it was a fact and her maid was in collusion with him—he'd not expect to find the pearls around her waist."

"But what else than that string of splendid pearls that Walsh wants traced, while I'm clearing his wife's name about the other, could have been the motive for her murder?" Sewell exclaimed. Pointer nodded in sympathy as he crossed to the window, where stood a little table with some letters and note-paper on it. An engagement-book lay at one side and Pointer looked up its last date. There was one entry for this same day. "4 o'clock," was scrawled in pencil, as though noted hastily.

"Nothing else?" queried Sewell, peering over Pointer's arm. "Four o'clock she was alive. Five she was alive. It's what happened between five and five-thirty that's the riddle! Look here," he cried, "say it was she herself who took some box out from that cabin trunk under her bed, at 'four o'clock.' The interview takes place then. She tears back here for her hidden pearls at five. . . ."

"—And didn't replace her keys in her handbag—but flung them into that drawer?" Again Pointer was clearly sceptical. He plainly could not see the owner of that bunch of keys leaving them behind her, carelessly tossed into a frail little drawer for safe custody.

CHAPTER TEN: THE FINGERPRINTS SEEM TO LINK UP THE KEYS WITH A CERTAIN PERSON

The two slipped, still unheard, downstairs and outside. Drawing the front door noiselessly shut, Pointer pressed the bell. He had to ring three times. But at last a parlourmaid opened it, murmured promptly that none of the family was in, and was about to close the door again when Pointer stopped her with an authoritative gesture.

"There's been an accident to Mrs. Walsh," he said. "I want to ask you a few questions."

"Lor', sir!" said the maid in shocked tones, but addressing Sewell as a gentleman who had lunched at the house a few hours before. "Lor', sir! Not a serious accident, I hope." As she spoke, the parlourmaid showed them in.

"Very serious. Fatal, I'm sorry to say. Mrs. Walsh is dead," was the reply. "How can we get into touch with her mother, Mrs. Finch-Gray?"

"Dead!" The maid turned shocked eyes on Sewell again. "Why you yourself, sir, lunched here with the mistress and master to-day! And she was in her bedroom around five! How did it happen, sir?"

"Head injury," was the reply. "She was killed outright."

"Oh, those cars!" the maid ejaculated. "What's the use of Belisha Beacons! Just inviting a body to step out and be run over! And Miss Vi always was in a hurry . . . always in a rush," she babbled on, too excited to pause. "I felt it in my bones that she'd be run over some day. And what Mr. Walsh will do, I can't think! Only married a few days, and fair doting on her! Oh, sir, it's dreadful! Her poor mother, too!"

"Yes, where can we find her mother?" Pointer asked sharply.

"She's not back in Town yet," the parlourmaid replied, shaking her head. "She's not expected back till dinner next Friday. Might I ask where the accident happened, sir?"

"In a place called Stanley Mews. Do you know it?" Pointer questioned.

"Mr. Gray owns some property there, I know. Was Mrs. Walsh there in her car?" But, not proposing to satisfy her avid curiosity:

"Were Mr. and Mrs. Walsh dining at home to-night?" Pointer asked instead of replying.

"No, sir. They were to dine with some friends of theirs."

"Who is Mrs. Walsh's personal maid?" was the next question. Upon which he was told that Mrs. Walsh was looking for one, but had not yet been satisfied. For the time being the parlourmaid valetted Mr. Walsh, and the housemaid looked after Mrs. Walsh.

The housemaid was fetched, was duly horrified at the "accident," and duly indignant at motor-cars.

"And when did you say Mrs. Walsh left the house this afternoon?" Pointer interpolated.

"About five, sir," was the positive answer, with a voluble account of "Mr. Mills' call" when "Mrs. Walsh had just gone out."

"You saw her go out?" Pointer asked casually, and was told that Gwendolyn herself had not. But when she heard her stirring around in her bedroom—as the maid had chanced to hear in passing it—she, Gwendolyn, had knocked and, on the door remaining shut when asked, through it, what the knock was for, had herself asked through it if Mrs. Walsh would like tea. On which she was similarly assured through the closed door, "No, thanks," in Mrs. Walsh's well-known voice.

Pointer's only comment was to ask where Mrs. Walsh kept her keys. The instant reply being, "She always carries them in her little handbag, just as Mrs. Finch always does."

"Her keys should be locked up, or handed to Mr. Walsh now," Pointer said. "Suppose you come up and see if you can't find them in her bedroom. Her handbag has been opened and there are no keys in it."

The two maids stared at one another. Both said that they had never known Miss Vi not to take her keys with her, and Gwendolyn led the way upstairs with the look of one who performs a requested act with no hope of success.

"Just glance through the drawers for them," Pointer directed; and, reiterating that Mrs. Walsh never went out without them, the maid pulled at a drawer at one side of the dressing-table. "She always locks everything, sir," the maid insisted. "She only left this drawer unlocked for me to put in it something that was coming from the shop. This one—" She opened it—and gave a cry. "But—these can't be Mrs. Walsh's!" the house-maid exclaimed, picking up the little bunch of keys that Pointer had replaced. "They can't be! Is this a joke, sir?" she asked suddenly and suspiciously.

"A joke? Why?" Sewell broke in to ask in his turn.

"Well, sir—seeing that I put those frills in there not half an hour ago myself and no keys were there then—of course it seems like some joke to find them on top of those very frills!"

"Look here," Pointer decided to explain, "I think you ought to know—both of you—that Mrs. Walsh's death is being investigated by the police. To clear up exactly how it happened. I am a detective inspector from New Scotland Yard—Mr. Sewell here will vouch for that—and I want you to tell me all that you can about her things."

Still, as was intended, the two maids only thought of Mrs. Walsh's death as happening in a car accident. They were too startled and shocked by the news itself to wonder at the questions they were asked.

"These came from Dickins and Jones this afternoon, sir," the housemaid who had acted as Mrs. Walsh's temporary maid explained. "Mrs. Walsh ordered them yesterday, and she told me that when they came I was to be sure and lay the frills carefully in this drawer, which she had left unlocked for them, so as not to let them get mussed at all. And to think of finding her keys—and they certainly do look like hers—right on top of them! But who in the world could have put them there, sir?" She eyed the two men searchingly. "For nobody's been in the house since I laid the frills in that drawer—except, of course, Mr. Mills when he called. And he went out again at once when he was told that Mrs. Walsh was not in."

"At what time, exactly, did you put them in the drawer and close it?" Pointer asked, taking out his note-book to show the importance of question and answer.

"Dickens and Jones delivered them close on half-past four, sir, and they were laid neatly in the drawer almost at once." It appeared that the housemaid had been quick about it, and knew just when she finished her task, because she wanted to slip out for a word with the young postman who collected letters at that time from the pillar-box nearby, and he couldn't wait long.

On her side, the parlourmaid had heard Mrs. Walsh back again in her bedroom just about 5 o'clock—when she, Gwendolyn, happened to be passing it. She was quite certain of that, for she knew "Miss Vi's" voice well, as also "her ways of stirring around in her room." She couldn't be mistaken about either thing. She had turned the tap on full in her fitted basin, too, which was her regular signal when she didn't want to bother to open her door. "Besides," she said triumphantly as to her certainty, "it couldn't have been any one else speaking." As for the time when Mr. Mills rang the front-door bell, the parlourmaid could be equally certain about that. For cook had just tuned-in for the North Ireland news from the B.B.C. at quarter-past five. So Mrs. Walsh must have come back for something and gone out again just before that. But none of the servants had noticed it, either time. Mr. Walsh had given the servants' hall a new and splendid wireless set, and they were "all crazy to listen to it."

Then Pointer had a few words to say as to how fresh and charming the bedroom looked; and was told about its having been newly decorated for the bridal pair's use of it until their own house could be done over for them. And, in reply to another word of praise, learnt that all the old pieces had been French polished just the day before their arrival. Oh, yes, including the dressing-table, of course.

The two men hurried out, making a great show of haste, so that they need not say more about the "accident." Outside in the car they jotted down the time-table thus obtained.

"About five o'clock she was heard in her room. By five-fifteen she was gone. Just before half-past five the telephone message reached her husband asking him to go at once to Stanley Mews. The three got there," noted Pointer, " ust past the half-hour, and found Mrs. Walsh murdered. We were notified a couple of minutes before quarter to six. The doctor saw the body at practically six o'clock, and, as the day is warm, puts the hour of death as around five at the very latest; although, if that time should be challenged he would be prepared to extend it backwards to four o'clock; but not to advance it. It looks, therefore, as though she must have been killed very soon after leaving her mother's house, as she was heard in her room at five . . . and it took us just eight minutes from door to door. I was careful, though, not to drive very fast, and we had the lights against us once so the journey could have been made in a lucky five minutes."

"It looks as though she had been killed at once on entering, or rather on returning to the flat in the Mews," Sewell said, jotting down this time-table. "But that four o'clock appointment . . .! Mr. Walsh evidently can't help us about that, and I must get to work sharply on his commission," he added as he slipped his note-book into his pocket. "And those pearls . . .! I must certainly have a

word with Miss Lovelace first of all, and hear her version
of the affair."

"Meanwhile," Pointer said, "the Yard will probably
establish whose fingerprints are on the drawer where the
keys were found. As also how long Mrs. Walsh was at her
dressmaker's in Bruton Street."

They parted with an agreement to dine together and
talk over the affair from any fresh angle obtained in the
interval.

On calling, Sewell learned that Miss Lovelace was in;
and, on being given the message he pencilled on his card,
she saw him at once.

She made a charming vision, too, in something all ice-
blue frills and a big pale rose bow of ribbon. Her face,
exquisitely made up, her coral-tinted cheeks showed no
pallor, but the pupils of her large eyes were enormously
dilated. So it seemed that even Miss Lovelace could feel
an emotional shock. Sewell had fancied her haughtily
impervious to any.

She had heard the dreadful news, she said, about half
an hour ago from her maid, who had heard it from one of
the maids with whom she was great friends at Friars
Halt. And much to his surprise, Sewell found Ann
Lovelace quite different from what he had expected. She
spoke gently and sympathetically of Arthur Walsh's
murdered bride, deploring her own previous thoughts
about her in connection with the imitation pearls which
the then Violet Finch had insisted on leaving with her as
security for the sum which Ann had advanced for the
other's gambling debt at the night-club the two had
visited out of curiosity.

And in return for what Sewell was touched by as
Ann's candour, he explained how he had come to call on
her for just such details as Arthur Walsh's private
investigator. "For I have no connection with the police, I
hope you know, Miss Lovelace—except as a personal
friend and admirer of Chief Inspector Pointer. But my
profession is the clearing up of wrongly-aspersed

reputations, and Walsh is determined to have his wife's honour vindicated."

"I do hope you'll be successful," Ann exclaimed impulsively. "I feel sure now, in cold blood, that she, too, had been somehow made the victim of that cleverly-substituted copy of the real string of pearls. And now you are going to find out, I hope and trust, who really did steal the original string, for I suppose it's stolen?" she asked. Adding eagerly: "In justice to that poor murdered girl it's all one can do now, and I'm only too glad to help.

"But why was she at that man Mills's flat? Can he be at the bottom of the mystery? Between you and me, Mr. Sewell, he looks capable of it! Handsome enough, well groomed, and all that, yet somehow a rank outsider. But then—of course!" Her embarrassed silence finished the sentence to the effect that Violet Walsh had been no less an arrant outsider, too.

Sewell just touched on Walsh's belief that it was in trying to find out something about the mystery that his wife had met her death. Ann said she was sure it must be the explanation.

They shook hands warmly, and Sewell was delighted at Miss Lovelace's acceptance of his invitation to lunch with him as soon as he should have learned more about the whole puzzling mystery.

Ann immediately drove down to Friars Halt, and arrived there to find Arthur closeted with the Colonel. Kitty saw her car arrive, but withdrew to her own rooms. Not that Ann asked for her, but seated herself in the library which opened out of the Colonel's den. And for once both girls had one and the same anxiety: What was going on in Colonel Walsh's study?

How was Arthur telling his dreadful news? How was his father taking it? Lady Monkhouse, Ann knew, was away, staying with friends.

In actuality the Colonel listened in horrified silence, aghast at Arthur's broken, stammered account of what had been found in Stanley Mews.

"Terrible! An incredibly dreadful affair!" he said finally in choking nightmare sensations.

"To think that Ann thought Violet knew about those pearls being false! She went to the Mews because she had learnt something," Arthur wound up. "Something linking the place with the stolen and imitated pearls—for that shorter string is missing. We haven't been able to find it anywhere."

His eyes on his knees, the Colonel made no comment. He did not see the affair in that light at all; and his absolute silence plainly said as much. At which Arthur, his head held very stiff and very high, took his wordless departure, encountering Ann Lovelace outside, as she had meant that he should. But a very different Ann from their last meeting.

He made as if to pass her, but she caught his elbow, appealing with trembling lips:

"Arthur, I've come to apologise—utterly and completely. I was all wrong! I was a jealous beast to her! This—this awful affair—" And with that he took her outstretched hand in his, holding it in eloquent silence for a long moment.

This was the picture that met Kitty Walsh as she came quietly down the stairs congratulating herself that Ann was now safely out of the way. And in the talk that followed—for Ann saw her and drew her irresistibly into it—even Kitty had to agree that it took a very suspicious person indeed to doubt Ann's words of sympathy and remorse. As for Arthur, he thanked her for her touching expressions about Violet, in a voice that shook. Kitty's sympathy he seemed to take for granted. Then he drove back at once to town and to Sewell's flat. Sewell was in, and expecting him.

"God, man!" Arthur said in a tone that moved his friend deeply, "how little we dreamed what was coming, when I asked you to find out the truth about those damned pearls! If only I had never heard of them! But as it is, you're out of the search now, Sewell, and I take it up myself. Not that I think for a moment that I can fill your shoes at it —but you know how you would feel yourself if you stood in mine, my dear fellow!"

Sewell could well imagine that. Suppose it had been Kitty Walsh murdered, for instance! "I don't want to step out of it, though," he said slowly. "I haven't done anything yet and no one likes to fall down on a job. There's work in it for you, too, Walsh. I'll get on to the chief inspector and put it to him."

After a little delay Pointer got the message, and promptly asked Walsh to join in; and since Sewell wanted to continue his special investigation of the double mystery of the two pearl necklaces, Pointer invited both men to dine with him at his rooms, Sewell, meanwhile, to post Walsh as to just how far the investigation had yet gone.

"Now about that 'four o'clock' date jotted down in your wife's note-book, Walsh," Sewell said, "have you no idea what it stood for? Where she was going besides to her dressmaker?"

Arthur made a hopeless negative gesture with his cigarette. "She only told me that she had a lot of fittings to get through, and then spoke of being 'occupied' till past five. I lumped the two together, and thought she had meant that she would be at the dressmaker's until five. But, on thinking back, I remember her making two sentences of it, or rather of them. I'm dead sure she was hot on the track of that cursed string that started all this awful business. She was terribly upset by Ann's incredible suspicions about herself. And naturally, if she thought she had a chance of catching the thief, she would have gone for him bald-headed! Vi was just that sort."

Something in his voice made Sewell ask point-blank, "Have you any suspicions yourself?"

Arthur's eyes met his full on. "I know! But I've no proof. He came to me red-handed, Sewell!"

"It'll be difficult to prove," Sewell said. The name of Mills was not mentioned. There was no need.

"By the way," Sewell said suddenly, "Pointer thinks that Father Walsh knows something. Your cousin was close beside the Mews this afternoon, just about the time."

"Ambrose!" Arthur stared at the other as though in dismay. "Ambrose!" he repeated again. "I hope to God the chief inspector's mistaken," he went on slowly. "Ambrose is a damned difficult fish to land. And he's refused from the first to do Violet anything like justice. He will never forgive her because she suggested our getting married in a registry office. And a jolly unselfish thing of her it was, too!"

"Rather!" Sewell agreed warmly, "most girls seem to think they're on the films that day, and that the longer train and the more bridesmaids they have, the greater their chances of getting a full press."

"I was only too thankful to her," Arthur continued frankly, "but it damned us both with Ambrose. And as, unluckily, I had asked him to marry us, he guessed instantly who had been the instigator of the registry wedding. I wonder why the chief inspector thinks Ambrose knows anything to the purpose?"

"He didn't say; but Pointer's not one to think things without good reason, you may rest assured."

"I'll have a talk at once with my cousin." Arthur rose as he spoke. "I haven't been to confession for ages. He's always reminding me of my remissness. I'll go now; and afterwards, in the glow of welcoming back the prodigal son, he'll be bound to open up and aid me under these awful circumstances. Till to-night, then, Sewell! I may learn something really important from him."

Arthur hurried away on his errand, but when Sewell met him on the steps of the house in Bayswater, where the chief inspector had his comfortable rooms, it was to see a very disappointed expression.

"He's in a Retreat!" Arthur exclaimed bitterly. "I couldn't even send a message in. And it's to last four days!"

"Annoying!" Sewell said sympathetically. "But would he admit it, if he knew anything that would help in the inquiry? Supposing, of course, that it was anything he had learnt by accident in the ordinary way. . . ."

"If it would help Violet, he'd let himself be drawn and quartered rather than speak," Arthur said fiercely. "And it is wanted to help her name at least. The only help we can give her now." His face worked convulsively and, turning round, he pressed the bell violently.

Pointer welcomed them, repeating that he would be very glad indeed of Arthur's assistance. They had learnt from the shop in question—if one could call anything so quiet and handsomely appointed a "shop"—that Mrs. Walsh had left it at quarter to four, and had seemed anxious not to be late for some engagement, even declining to complete her fitting, which she had postponed to eleven to-morrow morning, when they were to have some furs up from cold storage for her inspection. She had walked away on foot from the establishment, the commissionaire said, refusing his offer to call a taxi for her.

Upon which Arthur said that Violet almost never used a taxi, preferring the exercise of walking. "She went to the Mews, which is quite close," he said confidently. "She didn't have an 'engagement,' but, on the contrary, surprised some one there, as she surmised that she would. I feel certain that she fearlessly taxed whoever she found there with the theft of the pearls—and was instantly killed on the spot."

"No, no! She was back in Ennismore Gardens at five," Sewell reminded him.

"She went to the Mews, I tell you! Must have done so, because of some knowledge of what had happened to the pearls," Arthur repeated stubbornly. "And to silence her, to prevent her telling me that knowledge, she was murdered."

At this point the chief inspector produced a startling contribution to the talk. The fingerprints on the drawer in Mrs. Walsh's bedroom proved to be Mills's.

"Got him!" exulted Walsh. "And I feared he might slip through the net!"

But Pointer shook his head. "I'm afraid the affair isn't as simple as that, Mr. Walsh, although it looks as though it had been Mills who had flung the keys into the drawer after taking something out of the trunk under her bed."

"Then I don't see how he can explain such evidence away!" Sewell's tone was also unconsciously exultant. "When are you going to spring it on him, chief inspector?"

"When I know more," Pointer said succinctly. "There was something very important in that trunk, something that Mr. Mills was determined to get at all costs."

"When did he slip into the room?" Sewell wondered.

"He must have watched, and seen my wife go out at five," Arthur cogitated, speaking dreamily as though to himself, "and then let himself in, run up to our room and helped himself to whatever it was in that trunk that he wanted. It may have been something of his own. Nothing more likely."

"But how did he get possession of the keys?" Pointer queried.

"Could he perhaps have made some plausible excuse, and got them from Mrs. Walsh herself as she went out?" Sewell suggested.

"That is, at any rate, probably what Mr. Mills will tell us," Pointer said dryly. "Which is why I want nothing to be said about the fingerprints found on the front of the drawer, at this stage of the investigation."

"But I suppose you keep the drawer as vital evidence," put in Arthur anxiously.

"Oh, certainly! We have it safe at the Yard. Luckily, it is mahogany, and one quite sufficiently like it was easily obtained and fits the dressing-table well enough for ordinary notice," Pointer reassured him.

"Good!" Those particular fingerprints seemed to Arthur the first important piece of evidence that had come to hand, although they were apparently only connected with the trunk under the bed in the mind of the chief inspector, and Arthur did not attach much importance to that cabin trunk, which himself he had never even seen. But, whatever it had held, the prints might be of the greatest use in proving the case against Mills—a case which must unfortunately rest entirely on circumstantial evidence.

Of one thing Arthur felt sure, and that was that the wanted pearls were not and never had been in that trunk. He had seen Violet take them out and put them away too often to have any doubts on that point. Which was the reason why he hoped that the cabin-trunk under the bed would not distract the eye of the chief inspector from the really important line of inquiry; but Arthur did not think that this would happen, "not being quite a fool."

As a matter of fact, Arthur Walsh was no bad psychologist—a much better one than one would have guessed from his face. And he thought that Pointer was most emphatically not a man to be sidetracked. Besides, there was Sewell to count on—Arthur's own agent, whose job it was to solve the mystery of the false pearls and the disappearance of the real ones.

The telephone bell rang.

"Mills speaking." He had just found Mrs. Finch at Henley and had broken the news of the tragedy to her. She was terribly shocked and shaken. He, Mills, thought that she ought to have at least a night's rest and quiet. But Mrs. Finch insisted on seeing the officer in charge of the case at once. They were therefore driving back at once to Ennismore Gardens. Would the chief inspector manage to meet them there? Mills added that he had been asked by Mrs. Finch to stay there, as he was, of course, giving up his rooms in the Mews at once.

Chapter Eleven: A Mother's Grief Does Not Appear To Be Overwhelming

Mrs. Finch showed few outward marks of grief, to the chief inspector's apparently casual glance, when he followed Arthur Walsh and Sewell into the drawing-room at Ennismore Gardens. She looked surprised to see Pointer with them, but without expressing it otherwise.

She turned to Arthur with both hands outstretched. "I don't know how to say what I feel! Grief for poor Violet, and horror at the way of her death!"

He held her hands for a moment before gently seating her again, as he said brokenly, "I don't think any of us can express what we feel about it, except by doing all we can to help Scotland Yard to see to it that her murderer doesn't escape justice. Sewell, here, is helping, too—in his own expert way."

Mrs. Finch seemed puzzled at this, but she asked no question; and Sewell had been told by Arthur, on their way to Ennismore Gardens, that she presumably knew nothing about the loss of any pearls, which had made Sewell give him a somewhat astonished glance but, like Mrs. Finch now, he had asked no questions.

"The first of the lot that's a complete enigma to us," Arthur continued, "is, what could have taken Vi to Mills's flat?"

Mrs. Finch seemed to pause a moment before replying that, with Mills and herself away at Maidenhead, Violet might have made an appointment with some one there, thinking she would be sure to have the place to herself. Or, rather, knowing she would have—Mrs. Finch corrected herself. "For Mills and I were detained in Maidenhead all day until half-past four, when he agreed to buzz up to town for me, to ask Violet for some papers which I thought we ought to have. I know the exact time, because we compared our watches as to whether he could get them back to me within an hour and a quarter. It was just possible, if the road was clear both ways, and if Violet was quick about handing them to him."

If Mills had left Maidenhead at half-past four, he would only have just been able to reach Ennismore Gardens at a quarter past five. It was a complete alibi, if it could be depended on. One does not as a rule suspect a mother of giving a false alibi to any one who might have killed her daughter, but, apart from the fact that Mrs. Finch did not strike Pointer as being an ordinary mother, the man in question was her business partner, and he thought that, to this woman, the latter fact might outweigh everything else.

"And was your husband, Mr. Gray, with you?" Pointer asked now.

He was told that Mr. Gray was in Birmingham at a motor show there. He had been away some three days, and, except for this tragedy which would bring him home at once, would have been away for another three.

Pointer did not ask her as to what the relations had been between the stepfather and the dead woman. He did not ask what he called "capital" questions of close relations. Still less of a wife concerning her husband, or of a husband concerning his wife. They were "out of bounds" in his regular inquiries, necessitating other sources of the wanted information.

"Have you any idea how Mrs. Walsh's will runs?" he asked, instead, with a deprecating glance at Arthur.

Mrs. Finch shrugged her shoulders indifferently as she answered, "Arthur settled a very handsome allowance on her, but all that Violet owned to bequeath consisted of a couple of pearl necklaces and some other jewellery."

Pointer now nodded to Sewell, who then told Mrs. Finch under what circumstances he himself had been called in professionally by Walsh; and the latter amplified Sewell's statement by other relating details.

At this his mother-in-law sat very still. Her greedy lips sucked in at the corners, her small cold eyes intently fixing themselves now on Sewell, now on Arthur, as she listened with her whole being as well as with her ears.

"But that's the shorter string," she said when the latter had finished about the imitation necklace. "I won't stop to say how astounded I am at what you tell me. Arthur, you didn't breathe a word of all this to me! That was most considerate of you. But just like you, dear boy! And what about the longer string—the much more valuable necklace? Where is it?"

"It was not on Mrs. Walsh when she was found—dead," Pointer said.

"Well, of course, it must be traced! And the other one, too!" said Mrs. Finch firmly. "They were about all that the poor child had to leave, and it would grieve her terribly if she could know that her mother didn't even get that much!"

"Had Mrs. Walsh any known enemies?" Pointer asked. It was a stereotyped question; but he had never found one more initially useful in suggesting the trail or trails of those private enmities that surround so many a murder.

Mrs. Finch turned to her son-in-law. "Well, Arthur, what about it?" she asked him with an enigmatic smile. "You would know about that better than any one else could, wouldn't you?"

"Not necessarily," Arthur answered grimly, "until this mystery about the pearls is cleared up."

"Well, there you are, then! Who accused poor Violet of having known that the pearls were false just in order to stop the marriage? A most atrocious lie! But who particularly wanted to stop your marriage?"

"Do you mean my cousin, Ambrose Walsh?" Arthur asked coldly.

Mrs. Finch gave a derisive snort. "Try again!" she advised.

"Miss Lovelace—"Arthur began still more stiffly.

"Do you mean Ann?" snapped Mrs. Finch. "Well, what about Ann Lovelace? Violet had no greater enemy, you can bet on that!"

"Not now! Ann's most frightfully sorry for having so misjudged her," Arthur protested. "I can't tell you all the kind and true things she said remorsefully about Violet. I was most frightfully touched by her moving words, Mrs. Finch."

Mrs. Finch stopped him with an upraised finger, as though he had been a taxi. Her face was stony.

Pointer recognised that here was a nature as hard as adamant. This was a bereaved mother who exhibited a singular lack of feeling about her daughter's dreadful death. Indeed at times something approaching an actual dislike of Violet Walsh looked from Mrs. Finch's eyes, spoke in her tones, but never in her words.

"The first thing to do, as you say, Arthur, is to trace and produce those pearls of Violet's." And, blandly ignoring the fact that he had said nothing of the kind to her, she turned to Sewell and continued with emphasis:

"Mr. Walsh has engaged you to clear his murdered wife's good name from foul imputations, Mr. Sewell. And so do I! And if you find those pearls for me—for they're mine now—you'll discover who was my poor child's mortal enemy."

At this Pointer asked her explicitly, "Am I to understand you to affirm, madam, that your daughter, Mrs. Walsh, had no property to leave, apart from her pearl necklaces?"

"Nothing else, except a very small bank balance, so far as I know," was the decided reply. "My husband, Mr. Finch, left me practically penniless. I contrived to make a small fortune, however, but lost it all by misled investments. As for my clubs —I'm much afraid there's nothing left of them but enormous debts. But I really can tell you nothing more. Mr. Mills, as he is obliged to, now, is putting up at my house."

They knew this last fact already, as also that Mills was reported "not in." And the chief inspector requested "Mrs. Finch" to accompany Inspector Watts to the Yard, and there put in writing her claims to the said pearls, explaining that he himself must be elsewhere for the next hour or so.

Arthur, accordingly, said good-bye to her and left the house, with Sewell and Pointer. He drew a deep breath as the door closed behind them. "There's something about that woman," he began, then stopped. "My murdered wife seems to have infected me with some of her own sensations," he muttered. "She was secretly terrified of her mother." He turned to Pointer and they got into the latter's car. "It's a terrible thing to say, but I can't set her aside from this dreadful affair—at any rate as regards the pearls. Violet told me that she had been virtually forced to leave them to her in the will that she signed just the day before our marriage. Those damned pearls! But for them my poor girl would be alive now. Don't you think so, too?" he asked Pointer. At whose reply:

"So far, it certainly looks as though the pearls were closely connected with her death; but by the way, Mr. Walsh, who would inherit from you in the event of your own death?"

Sewell looked surprised, and Arthur stared.

"I suppose the bulk of my father's fortune would go to Ambrose Walsh, my cousin the priest," he said, "now that Gerald is dead—or even if he were alive, as anything that I have to bequeath will go to Father Walsh."

Pointer now heard about the priest's "Retreat," which had only just started. And he also learnt about the disinheriting of Arthur's elder brother, Gerald Walsh, and the reasons for it.

Pointer's next question referred, however, to the pearls in question. He asked how, and from whom, Mr. Walsh had first heard of them. Arthur had to think hard back for a moment, before he recalled that it had been "Miss Lovelace" who had told him of two remarkably beautiful pearl necklaces that had belonged to the unfortunate Queen Charlotte of Mexico, and which she knew were for sale at a price that was really "a bargain" for such pearls. But he added that he could by no means feel sure that that was "the first mention made about them, nor just who had originally put the idea into his head that the two strings would make a superb wedding gift to his bride. And Pointer let the query rest at this tragedy-obscured, vague remembrance of that detail.

Instead, he turned to the question of the larger and much more valuable string. "Mrs. Finch seemed to think, just now, that it might be in your safe. Is it there? I noticed that you let her suppose that you would turn it over to her after the reading of Mrs. Walsh's last Will and Testament."

"Of course it's in Violet's jewel box, in her mother's house," Arthur said. "That was why I did not argue with her about it."

On which Pointer glanced at his watch as he said, "Mrs. Finch promised to go to my rooms at once, so if you'll turn round, Mr. Walsh, we might see if the longer string is there now."

"You don't share Walsh's suspicion that Mrs. Finch may know something about the missing string, do you, chief inspector?" Sewell asked in a whispered aside as Arthur's attention was momentarily concentrated on passing between two drays.

"She's a most difficult woman to read—or surprise," Pointer replied. "But I think she has a distinct theory as to the identity of the murderer. A theory which she has not passed on to us. It was in existence before she heard about the loss of the pearls—and it does not centre on Miss Lovelace, I feel quite sure."

Chapter Twelve: An Advertisement is Found in Duplicate

Back at the house the three men learned that Mrs. Finch had summoned a taxi and driven to the Yard; police watch being maintained as to Mills's movements.

Arthur opened the door with his latch-key and Pointer and Sewell followed him into the house. Some tampering with the seals over the lock of the bedroom was evident to the chief inspector; but as they were intact he said nothing. And as soon as they were in the room Arthur opened the trunks with Violet's keys.

In the larger wardrobe trunk was her jewel-box. He unlocked that too, and with a sigh lifted out some really beautiful jewellery which had been partly wedding presents and partly gifts bought by him for his young bride on their honeymoon. Then he came to an oval flat leather box that had her initials in gilt on its lid. The pearls were in this, he said, and pressed the button. Inside lay a beautiful string of pearls; creamy white, with just the suspicion of a rosy gleam in their exquisite colour. "Yes, this is the larger string. So it's only the smaller that's missing," Arthur said as he lifted it out carefully.

"Are you sure they're genuine?" Sewell and Pointer asked simultaneously.

Walsh smiled as he let the string swing a little from his extended fingers.

"Don't they speak for themselves?" he replied, his voice movingly sad. Sewell felt in wordless sympathy.

Pointer was not an adept in the language of pearls. He modestly disclaimed the authority of an expert, but both a long experience in analogous cases and his lessons from jewel experts had taught him that genuine precious stones, and especially genuine pearls, have a peculiar and (he should say) quite inimitable coldness to the touch which he was inclined to think was not convincingly evident in this handsome string. An instant recourse to an unquestionable pronouncement, as to whether or not his own doubts were valid, was therefore a vital necessity in the present investigation. And in another minute the three men were seated in Pointer's car, taking the string for the judgment of the jewellers from whom Arthur, still reiterating that any doubt of its identity was incredible, had purchased the two necklaces as his wedding gift to Violet Finch.

On the chief inspector's card being sent in to him with an "urgent" request for his opinion, the manager had the three at once shown into his room. And had no sooner glanced at the necklace, even before it lay in his palm, than he unhesitatingly pronounced it "false." Adding:

"A marvellously deceptive imitation of the well-remembered and, of course, accurately recorded larger string of the two 'historically unique' pair sold to Mr. Walsh, here. This amazingly perfect copy is from Paris. The patent is the successful invention of a man named d'Erlanger, instances of whose genius in that line I have seen before; but none so astonishingly good. It is an expensive process; entirely mechanical; the copied pearls being turned out exact in weight, and very closely approximate in tint and even in apparent substance."

"How much would such an imitation as this one cost?" Pointer asked.

"At the present rate of exchange I could get it done, in the trade, for say—sixty pounds."

Walsh now held out the smaller string which Violet Finch had taken from Ann Lovelace. He had got her on the honeymoon to give them to him. Hung beside the other, even to his eyes, they showed as from one process.

Receiving a similar pronouncement, and Pointer having expressed his official thanks, a very silent and variously ruminating trio returned to the house, where a careful and thorough search of all the murdered bride's things failed to discover the other missing string.

Pointer requested Mr. Walsh to unlock the cabin trunk under the bed, and that also was searched. He called Arthur's attention to the space free in the otherwise stuffed tray. A metal despatch box? he queried. But Arthur said that he had never seen his wife in possession of such a thing. "Did she ever put the pearls into a hiding-place of her own devising?" Pointer asked. "Or rather, I should have asked if she ever hid 'the beads' thus. For it's conceivable, Mr. Walsh, that, as the shorter string was imitated before your marriage, the longer one may also have been changed then, and all the real pearls stolen at the same time."

Arthur made an unhappy gesture. "I'd say 'who cares?' " he replied bitterly, "in face of her death. But for the fact that clearing up about the cursed things means getting at the bottom of her mysterious death and, let us hope, hanging her murderer! But the more I think back to it—and I can't think about much else—I can't hold to my first hasty idea that it was he who phoned so urgently to me to go at once to the Mews. I believe now that, on the contrary and surely much more probably, that message that I stupidly took for a hoax was sent to save my darling from him! That it must have been the frantic effort of some one who had seen and recognised the wretch, perhaps as he was furtively stealing into the house or the flat. And if he happened to believe him one of a thieving gang that would stick at nothing to cover up their tracks, and then saw Violet go in and knew of our sensational marriage, that wildly confused message to me would be quite understandable, especially if she wasn't seen again coming out. Oh! to think," Arthur chokingly repeated, " that had I jumped into a car at once I might have saved her."

Sewell, however, tried to comfort those impassioned and vain regrets by again recurring to the alternative possibility that whoever sent that telephone message did it to keep the husband away from Mrs. Walsh's bedroom in Ennismore Gardens while it was ransacked for the larger string of pearls.

"It was at twenty-five past five," Arthur said more calmly and thoughtfully. "Yes, of course, that's a less torturing possibility. For—but for Mills—I might have come back . . . But then! But for Mills . . ." He stood staring down at the trunk fixedly when a tap on the locked room door startled him. "Mr. Walsh wanted on the telephone "; at which he slipped out of the room.

It was Ann Lovelace telephoning. She had been told that Arthur had gone with the chief inspector and Mr. Sewell to Ennismore Gardens; and she was "irrepressibly keen to learn" whether they had yet found the longer string of pearls, or had got on the track of the imitated shorter one, she said.

Arthur suggested that she should come herself to Ennismore Gardens, as he did not care to telephone the latest piece of news, which was "decidedly and most amazingly unexpected."

Whereupon Ann eagerly replied that she would be there in five minutes. She did it in less, and convulsively held Arthur's hand clasped tightly in both of hers as he told her of the finding of what he had of course supposed to be the longer string; of the chief inspector's doubts of its genuineness and their consequent immediate visit to the jewellers; the manager of whom had pronounced it false.

"Imitation!" she gasped. "Then both were imitation? Incredible!"

Arthur's fullest reply was his invitation to Ann to "come upstairs and see it." He brought her in with him and Pointer acquiescently showed her the string. Expressing her amazement, she repeated that of course Violet had been deceived as any one might well be! . . . "But where are the real pearls?" she looked about her inquiringly. And, as no one answered, she continued with fresh suggestions. "I wonder if any well-known purchaser was buying pearls just then? . . . They might have been bought quite innocently, I should think. Though I was rather thinking of the East. . . . There they adore pearls, don't they? . . . But may I have a hunt, too? It seems so absolutely impossible that they are not here somewhere."

As she spoke Ann opened the little drawers. Pointer and Sewell frankly watched this proceeding. Miss Lovelace seemed arrested by some scraps of printed paper. Not one came her way that she did not carefully glance through, however crumpled. Letters or papers with handwriting on it were also examined, but the chief inspector had an idea that she wanted to see if she could find something definite in print which had been kept by Violet Walsh and stuffed away in some inconspicuous place.

Pointer had with him the handbag which had been found in the room where Violet Walsh had been murdered. He had had its sides protected by transparent paper when handling it to see whether it would fit and fill the space left empty by some such article's removal from the trunk-tray under the bed. He thought it rather larger than the said space. Neither Ann nor either of the maids had ever seen it in Mrs. Walsh's possession. Evidently bought before her wedding, it was decidedly larger than any usually carried by Violet; less flat-sided on compression. In other words, capable of holding more in it.

Giving it, consequently, a fresh and still more thorough investigation with gloved fingers, Pointer now discovered a sort of secret division within it. For what looked and (casually) felt like an outside "side," exactly resembling the other side, even when seen from within when the bag was opened to use the rest of it, was, in reality the cover of a virtually "secret" division. This was completely masked to the eye by an inner lining-covered wire frame of serviceable firmness which so fully and exactly fitted into the "side" as to make a really undetectable division unless found by a knowing or a "searching" pressure on it: to "pry-out" the fitting beneath the outward catch closing the bag.

At first sight this "secret" division seemed to contain nothing. But on feeling down inside a flat-looking little pocket that had originally held a tiny mirror, in all probability, Pointer found a crumpled newspaper cutting.

It looked like a "personal," and ran:

Secretary of Rajah now in England wants to buy for his employer some really fine sapphires and pearls. Good prices given. A box number followed.

He glanced up casually, midway through it. Mr. Walsh was apparently oblivious of all but a letter which he was reading and reluctantly finishing before laying it down thoughtfully. But Miss Lovelace had her eyes fixed on the paper in the chief inspector's hand with a satisfied and exultant gleam in her eye. She had forgotten caution for the moment. Clearly Ann Lovelace knew the tenure of that scrap of print, the chief inspector silently noted, debating among his mental decisions the possibility of her having been exclusively searching for precisely this particular bit of evidence, and what that might mean.

He put the scrap back as though not especially interested by it, and leaving the bag carelessly on the table, turned to investigate also some books beside him.

After a minute or so he saw Miss Lovelace pick up the bag and begin to examine it. In an adjacent mirror he covertly kept an eye on her, and presently, as he had confidently expected, heard her give a surprised little cry:

"Arthur! Just look! . . . But no: I don't see that it helps us. . . ." She turned a charming, friendly, puzzled face to him.

"What did you find?" Arthur asked eagerly, and Pointer permitted himself to look interested. So did Sewell.

"Oh, it's only an advertisement that Violet seems to have cut out and forgotten," Ann said vaguely. "I found it in this side pocket of her handbag. It's an offer to buy any specially good pearls or sapphires. . . . She had such splendid examples of both, that such an advertised offer would catch Violet's eye, of course. But she wouldn't cut it out for that. Yet she did cut it out. I wonder if she thought her stolen string of pearls had been sold to the advertiser!"

Arthur looked puzzled and disappointed by her "big cry and little wool." He handed the cutting back to her almost irritably. "I don't see that that's any help! It's much too far-fetched. Why should Vi connect that with her less valuable string of pearls? For she didn't know the bigger and much finer string was missing, or I should have been told of it at once."

"Of course you would have been!" Ann agreed heartily. "I thought of that too, Arthur, after my first hasty hope that it might be a really helpful clue. But on reflection there's this to be thought of: Violet kept the advertisement. Why?"

Arthur, however, shook his head with a gesture that had a hint of fresh impatience in it, but Ann continued:

"For some good reason, you may be sure!" She spoke with certainty. "Kept it here in her handbag to be able to refer to it. I feel absolutely certain, Arthur, that she knew something that suggested a link between her pearls and this rajah's secretary."

Pointer now requested to see the cutting again. Sewell, too, studied it with a falling countenance. It looked bad for the innocence of Mrs. Walsh, his client. To establish her guiltlessness was his job.

"It's quite a suggestion, Miss Lovelace," Pointer said gravely to her. "But if Mrs. Walsh had any reason to link this cutting with her missing necklace it would mean that it appeared after she knew that she had pledged you an imitation string."

At his words, Walsh looked the first time as though there might be something in Ann's idea. She looked from him to Pointer, and again forgot her mask. For her eyes showed the same exultant, cruel gleam they had betrayed when they had fallen, earlier, on the scrap he had just discovered.

"Oh, of course," she said lightly. "The date of the cutting will be quite easy to trace, I should think."

"Quite easy," Pointer endorsed. "It's from the Daily Wire, I think; or rather, I'm sure. Should it transpire that there really is some vital connection between it and the wanted pearls, you'll have been no mean ' link' yourself, Miss Lovelace, in pointing it out."

"Oh no!" Ann looked as though that tribute would not at all meet with her approval. "It was Mrs. Walsh who had the cutting and you who found it, chief inspector. It's nothing to do with me at all; but if I have chanced on anything that will clear her name from my mistaken charge against her, oh, I shall be relieved and thankful, Arthur!" she exclaimed remorsefully, turning to him with shining eyes, at the sympathy of which he looked deeply touched.

"Here are some of Mrs. Walsh's letters that should be glanced through," Pointer interrupted. He himself had already done so. "Mr. Walsh, would you take them into one of the downstairs rooms and just run over them? And perhaps Miss Lovelace would help you with them," he added suggestively.

Ann repeated that she would be glad to help; and the door was closed behind the two.

Pointer locked it and produced on the instant, from under his arm, a charming flat lizard-skin pocket. It was Ann Lovelace's. He had picked it up from a chair where it had accidentally fallen, and trusted to the circumstance that, with her hands over-full of papers and envelopes, she would not miss it at once.

He went through it with dexterous quickness. There were no bloodstains on it, or on anything in it. But in a closed central division, separately fastened with its own little catch, was the same cutting as the one which he had found in the dead woman's handbag. Replacing this cutting in every way exactly as and where he had found it, Pointer laid the bag down again where it had been dropped, unlocked the door of the room and continued his searching inspection of everything in the room.

A few minutes later Ann and Arthur came back with the examined papers of Mrs. Walsh, none of which, Arthur assured Pointer, could have any bearing on the case. And Ann, after a startled expression on catching sight of her own handbag, seized it hurriedly and went off with Arthur to find out the date of the newspaper cutting, promising to telephone it at once to the other two.

Sewell broke the pregnant silence that followed this departure by murmuring with a frown:

"So Miss Lovelace had a similar cutting! I only hope the date . . ." He left the sentence unfinished, substituting: "I wish I felt as certain of Mrs. Walsh's good faith as Miss Lovelace is."

" 'Is'? Or professes to be?" queried Pointer dryly.

"She did purr a bit, didn't she?" Sewell said disconsolately. "I'm not so sure about her own good faith as I was. What with one thing and another, I shouldn't be surprised if Miss Lovelace had herself contrived, for some reason of her own, to slip the tell-tale scrap into the handbag carried by Mrs. Walsh—or Miss Finch—for it might have been done before the wedding." Sewell's brow contortions were an index to his perplexed cogitations as he added: "Chief inspector, do you suspect some such spiteful trap to eventually snare Walsh's fiancee—or bride? Or do you believe the latter was responsible for it?"

Pointer, however, refused to be drawn into any more explicit pronouncement, at this stage of an extremely complicated investigation, than his tersely non-committal reply: "Either might be so."

Chapter Thirteen: Evidence Accumulates

Sewell's professional interests were at issue as well as his disinterested concern for his friend. The latter maintained that the cutting only proved what he had claimed from the first: that his wife had come on something which had linked the fraudulent necklace directly with Mills's flat, if not with Mills himself. But Sewell now had disturbing doubts, which must be settled, pro or con, so that, while he half-wished that he had not accepted the commission, the other half of his mentality knew that he did not want to relinquish the intriguing problem unsolved.

If the living Violet had been what her adoring husband thought her, what she had as convincingly appeared to be, at that luncheon, then that cutting should help him to establish it. It might, he thought, lead either to Mills or to some one connected with her mother's circle. For it had been while Violet was again living under her mother's roof that she had gone on some suspicion to the Mews, and been murdered in consequence.

Significant, too, was the fact that she had chosen a day for her visit to the fiat when she would have every reason to think that neither her mother nor Mills would be in it. Mrs. Finch's theory that her daughter had gone to meet some one else there had been put forward very quickly. Was it her honest belief? These were questions that Sewell wanted more light on. And it teased him, as well as humiliated his professional pride, to think that what was all fog to him might be fairly clear to the chief inspector; and that not so much from superior training as from keener deductive insight.

"Where do you suggest that one should seek for clues, if not actual evidence, in this case?" he asked him. He did not look for direct assistance, but it would be well to learn along what avenues Pointer's intentions were moving.

"I think the two families concerned should be closely studied as important factors," Pointer answered. But Sewell could not quite get at the kernel in this nut. He was too tired to crack it at this late hour, and with a murmured "Good-night" the two separated.

Next morning Sewell was at breakfast when Pointer rang him up to say: "I've some news that will interest you. Walsh is still asleep, his man says, but if you care to come round—"

Sending instantly for his car, in a very short time Sewell was seated at Pointer's breakfast-table, where he completed the meal abandoned at his own place. That speedily done, the chief inspector handed him a note that he had received a few minutes earlier. It was from the fingerprint department at Hendon.

"You remember those bits of torn-up paper that were found around the murdered Mrs. Walsh's feet?" Pointer said.

"Yes. Quite blank, I understood. Weren't they?" Sewell asked eagerly.

"Well, I had them tested for fingerprints," Pointer said. "You can't tear paper up easily with gloves on. And our powder showed some marks on those."

"Fingerprints! Whose?" exclaimed his listener.

"Four clear fingerprints were found on them and traced to one of the men working in the garage. But all the others are those of Mr. Mills," Pointer answered.

"They were bound to be!" interjected Sewell. "His flat; his prints! But what about the garage man? Was there an accomplice in the murder?"

"Not necessarily. I have already had a few words with the mechanic in question, before I met you on the front doorstep here. I asked him whether any parcels had recently come for Mr. Mills, and if so, who had taken them in. That torn blank paper was wrapping-paper. He explained that the three gentlemen living in the house usually answered their own door-bells. But if they were out, and parcels or registered letters came, they were left at the garage with whoever was in charge there at the moment. And yesterday, he told me, a little package had come for Mr. Mills from his laundry, about three in the afternoon. The man who brought it said it was a handkerchief that had been left out of Mr. Mills's things sent home at the end of last week."

"Around three." Sewell was pale with excitement. "If that's so . . . Then how did the paper—you think it was that wrapping-paper, of course— but how did it come to have Mills's fingerprints on it? He says he didn't go over to his flat at all yesterday until he went there with Miss Kitty and Arthur Walsh at half-past five."

"Exactly!" Pointer replied. "That's the question, and an important one. Inspector Watts has one of the pieces of paper with him—to match it at the laundry, if possible. I rang them up on the telephone this morning and asked particulars of the handkerchief sent."

Sewell did not quite see why; but he said nothing.

"The manageress told me that it was of bright blue silk, with large white spots on it."

"Mills did have one of that description thrust up his cuff yesterday, when we saw him at his flat!" Sewell threw out his hand with quite a dramatic gesture. "But that would mean?"—his face was all puckers. "How could you prove it was the same handkerchief?"

"Quite possibly he won't be carrying it to-day," Pointer said. "At least one would expect him to use only subdued colours just now. And if it can be got hold of, among his things, and the laundry can recognise it positively as the one they sent home to him yesterday in the early afternoon by special delivery, Mr. Mills would need to exercise all his ingenuity to explain it away."

"If it can be got hold of! But how can it be done?" Sewell persisted.

"Say a man, claiming to be from the laundry, calls and asks one of the maids in Ennismore Gardens not to get him into trouble, but to let him have it back, for it wasn't Mr. Mills's, but belonged to another customer. He adds that he's bringing back the right blue and white one instead. Say the maid, touched by his good looks and his pleading, gives him back from Mr. Mills's room the one sent to Mr. Mills's flat yesterday. Say the laundry identify it? . . ."

"If the laundry identify that handkerchief—as they will—you'll have him!" Sewell exclaimed. "But his alibi? It was confirmed by the mother of the murdered woman! Are you going to question her about that, Chief Inspector?"

"Mrs. Finch is too ill to see any one this morning," Pointer replied with a very unsympathetic look at his companion. "It happens to fit in well with some of her commercial difficulties—not to be able to reply to questions for some days—so I don't think she'll recover in a hurry."

"But surely, to catch her daughter's murderer!" the other expostulated. "Are you going to arrest Mills, or question him first?" he asked.

"Question him, assuredly. But at this juncture —only about his fingerprints in her room," was the firm reply. Which evoked from Sewell almost a groan.

"Then where, my dear chief inspector, does my commission come in? That scrap of paper we found, or rather those two scraps, seemed the first practical suggestion of where to hunt for the pearls that I've come across yet! And what, may I ask, do you make of Miss Lovelace's possession of its duplicate?"

"Just what you yourself make of it, I fancy," was the smiling reply. "For obviously, if Miss Lovelace hadn't found that cutting in Mrs. Walsh's bag on some previous opportunity, her whole bearing showed that she knew of its existence; even if she had not determined that one of the two cuttings should be found there when we were searching for 'evidence' of any sort whatsoever."

"Yes; I begin to think Miss Kitty Walsh was right: that Miss Lovelace isn't the simple transparently kind creature I took her to be." Sewell's gloom brightened a little as he added the indulgent rider: "Of course, just now, she's trying to get Walsh on the rebound from his grief over his wife's awful death. And she may! He's tremendously touched, I know, by her remorseful way of sympathising in his determination to hound down her murderer."

Pointer was now wanted on the telephone. The torn-up paper had been identified as the same that had been used to deliver the handkerchief to Mills from his laundry yesterday.

"And the handkerchief will prove that it was in the flat early yesterday afternoon," Sewell said. "I wonder though . . . Mrs. Walsh was here at five. Could she have torn that paper into bits? Did it also serve to wrap up the pearls? Frankly, Pointer, I'm at sea! Absolutely at sea!"

Pointer made no comment.

"The date when that advertisement was inserted," Sewell continued after another gloomy interval, "may get us one step forward."

"A big one at that," Pointer agreed, "though not necessarily in the direction you desire, my dear fellow," was his unspoken reflection before Sewell resumed:

"And what about Mills's gloves?"

"Mr. Mills's outfit in that respect would seem to have consisted of two pairs only. Both pairs quite uninteresting," said the chief inspector.

"But did one glove look crumpled? As though it had been forced into an inner waistcoat pocket?" Sewell asked with intense interest.

"You expect too much. The fault of youth!" was the smiling response. "Both pairs looked smooth, and very little used."

"Humph!" was Sewell's discontented ejaculation. "But, by the way, where was Colonel Walsh yesterday afternoon?"

"I dropped in late last night at Friars Halt, as I happened to be in the neighbourhood." Pointer threw in this last explanatory clause quite casually. It was, however, received with a derisive grin.

"He spent yesterday afternoon, he says, looking through a very well-known bulb importer's stock. From half-past three to well past five."

"Anyway, I don't see Colonel Walsh battering-in the head of even an unwelcome daughter-in-law," Sewell called over his shoulder as he hurried off.

At the Yard Pointer was informed that Mr. Mills was back and quite at his service if the chief inspector would like a talk with him. Upon which Pointer phoned asking Mills to make the immediate interview in his official room. And when his visitor was shown in it was with a very haggard countenance that he seated himself.

Pointer wasted no time in skirmishing. He asked him point-blank how he accounted for the fact that his fingerprints were found on a drawer of Mrs. Walsh's dressing-table.

Mills stared, and said he couldn't explain it at all, except that on the day before her return he had noticed that one of the drawers stuck out, and had thrust it home when Mrs. Finch showed him the room ready for the young couple. Obviously, he said, Violet had used the knob when opening and shutting it. As for the french-polishing—well, evidently the polisher had scamped his work. It was a possible explanation and it was made with apparent carelessness. Yet it might be the last talk the chief inspector could have with him without having to preface it by the warning which sounds so simple, aud which means so much,—the warning which a police officer is bound to give if he thinks the answers to his questions may mean an immediate arrest, that anything the questioned man or woman says will be taken down, and may be used in evidence.

Half an hour later Pointer learnt that the handkerchief had been definitely identified by Mills's laundry as the one sent by hand yesterday afternoon. The vanman had left it on his way to his own home, about half-past three; for he had driven away from the laundry at three and got home at four. And the Mews was almost exactly half-way by road between the two places.

So now there was definite evidence that Mills had been in his flat before four o'clock yesterday afternoon; and Mrs. Finch must be aware that she was giving him a false alibi unless her partner had misled her in some clever way. Pointer's mind, however, set that question aside for the moment to concentrate on other details of Mills's dossier.

Sewell meanwhile had contrived an interview with Miss Kitty Walsh, in which he told her of Miss Lovelace's change of heart towards Mrs. Walsh's implication in the false string of pearls.

"Change of heart!" Kitty shook her head like a mettlesome little filly. "Change of plan, more like, since she discovered that Arthur won't tolerate the least aspersion on Violet's good faith. I think Ann hopes to take her place as his consoling wife yet." Kitty spoke with careful lightness. "But she hates Violet, if possible more poisonously than ever. Don't make any mistake about that! For if you keep that fact before you, and read everything she says or does by its illumination, you may read Ann Lovelace correctly. Otherwise you, too, will be her dupe."

"You're a pretty good hater yourself, Miss Walsh," Sewell said with a grin. "That means a forthright nature."

"It means that I can't stand scheming. I'm a Walsh, too, remember!"

"Umph! I wish I could be as confident as to my own professional course towards my client," he said gravely. "I wish I felt sure that Walsh's fiancee and bride was all that he—" Sewell checked himself; his monkey's brow knotting itself up over conflicting responsibilities.

"I believe you're yourself falling into Ann Lovelace's net!" Kitty expostulated. "Oh, don't let her twist you round her finger, as she does Arthur, with her sham remorse and devotion to Violet's good name; her pretended belief, now, that Violet

was honest in pledging those pearls. Which simply means that she feels she can afford to talk generously because she has all the strings in her hand, to pull them the way she is after."

"You don't do my supposed intelligence justice," Sewell said smilingly. "We found something this morning (I don't feel at liberty to speak out about it), and I myself have a strong suspicion that Miss Lovelace may have somehow arranged for us to find it."

"Something that would tell against Violet?" Kitty asked.

"That's still uncertain," he admitted. "But it may! Damnably. Decisively, as far as I am concerned in the case."

Sewell was late for lunch with the chief inspector. But what he then heard was so enthralling to him that it actually put even Miss Kitty Walsh out of his thoughts for the time being, as he exclaimed:

"So it is all up with Mills!"

"I don't go as far as that," Pointer replied. "But we know, now, that he was in his flat before Mr. Walsh found his wife dead, murdered, there. We know that it was Mills's fingers that tore into shreds the bits of paper that we found at her feet; and that the handkerchief we saw in his pocket did not reach his rooms till half-past three."

Sewell looked at him with a furrowed brow. "But why should he put those scraps there? Why? They were all blank!"

Pointer did not reply. The question was rhetorical.

"And the marks on the drawer in her room?"

Pointer looked at his shoes. "They are suggestive, aren't they," he said. "But his explanation is—" He gave it, and Sewell passed a tired hand over his perplexed expression.

There was a ring on the telephone. Pointer was some time at it, apparently giving and receiving measurements concerning a carpet, while Sewell bobbed up and down on his chair like a cork dancing on waves.

"It's about the newspaper cutting," Pointer was beginning, when he was again interrupted by a telephone calling for the chief inspector.

"The cutting in Mrs. Walsh's handbag is to the fore," he said. "The first message to me, just now, was phoned from the Yard. The second was from Mr. Walsh and Miss Lovelace. Both bring the same authentic information; and I fear you will not be pleased by it.

"We learn that the advertisement was originally posted to not only the Daily Wire, from which the cutting was taken, as you know, but to all the other big London dailies severally; in each case with a prepayment enclosed for its insertion daily for a week, and giving a box number for replies to it."

"And the date when it was posted?" Sewell asked feverishly.

"Nearly a week before Miss Finch, as she was then, got Miss Lovelace to advance the money for her gambling debt, giving her alleged pearls as security for the loan," Pointer said gravely.

"So my murdered client could well have seen it!" Sewell said with a face no less significantly grave than was the chief inspector's.

"Mr. Walsh's message was more than a trifle incoherent," Pointer continued. "He says he realises what the facts must suggest; but begs 'earnestly' to 'suspend judgment for later data.'"

"Who sent it and paid for the advertisement?" Sewell asked.

"The sender gave his name as 'Mr. Elwes Morris,' and the ' Cumberland Hotel' as the address from which he wrote. Each daily which had inserted it received quite a number of replies. Some are still being received; although Mr. Morris sent instructions to each paper to forward nothing more 'as he was leaving.' And he did leave at the end of his week. Seemed quite the usual hotel guest, the manager of the Cumberland says. Had no servant with him, very little luggage, and occupied one of their smaller and less expensive rooms.

"Shall we go on there?" Pointer asked. They had not finished lunch, but neither man stayed for that, as they reached for their hats and gloves. Each wanted to be away before the husband could catch them up. The husband with his belief in his dead wife about to receive a final blow.

At the end of a couple of hours' inquiries they were aware that Mr. Elwes Morris, on leaving the Cumberland, had gone for a couple of days to the Regent Palace Hotel. He had had many telephone calls and many visitors at both hotels. He had used taxis exclusively. Had never dined in either hotel, and never used the public rooms. He suffered from a bad cold while at both places and always wore a muffler when passing to and fro.

"Disguised," Sewell said.

The chief inspector nodded vaguely.

"Surely—don't you think?" Sewell persisted.

"Oh, yes." But Pointer added nothing to the monosyllable. They then discussed the plans for the afternoon. Pointer wanted to go carefully over the events of yesterday with Kitty Walsh, in case she had noticed anything more than she had mentioned, and arranged with her to see her down at Friars Halt later in the afternoon. Meanwhile he intended to break the news to Mrs. Finch that the pearls on which she was counting were all imitation, and that the real ones were missing.

Sewell said that he knew the manager of the bank which Mills used, and he would try to see if he could glean from him a few friendly (as distinct from official) facts about the latter.

"And what about Colonel Walsh's alibi?" he asked as he was rising. "You know he made a selection of some of the newer daffodils, and then asked to be left alone in the shed where the commoner sorts of lily bulbs are kept."

"He often does that, it seems," responded Pointer. "Lets himself out by one of the doors used by the staff, and sends in his order when he has had time to think it over well and take counsel with his head gardener. That happened yesterday, it appears. He was alone from about four o'clock on. No one knows when he left. He himself says 'close on five'; and that he 'sat a while in the park afterwards.'"

"No alibi at all then," summed up Sewell. "It's lucky for him that the Colonel is really beyond suspicion." With which presumptive certificate Sewell sprinted for his car.

CHAPTER FOURTEEN: AN ALIBI GOES WEST

Pointer phoned to Mrs. Finch, explaining that he had news about the pearls which she ought to be told immediately. As he hoped, he was asked to come at once to Ennismore Gardens.

She was sitting before a writing-table littered with papers. She looked a very cool, level-headed business woman, not at all a bereaved mother.

Seating himself beside her, Pointer told her about the real pearls being, at present, untraceable; about the imitations substituted in their stead; about the report of the jeweller from whom they had been purchased; about the advertisement that had been cut from the Daily Wire; about the fingerprints of Mills on Violet Walsh's bedroom drawer, and also on the shredded-up scraps of paper found at her feet. "Torn up and strewn there after she was murdered," he said frankly. "Some of them are lying on spots of blood, yet none have bloodstains on them."

His aim was to move forward at least one step, by clearing away the alibi for Mills. An alibi which he showed Mrs. Finch was quite impossible. But she needed no showing. Her face changed as she heard about the pearls being missing, about the will being torn up. But when he came to the account of Mills's fingerprints it turned into the really dreadful face that Mrs. Finch could show when infuriated. And for a while she sat grasping the writing-table and swearing under her breath. Then she looked up at him with flint-like eyes.

"So that was his game, was it! And he's got the pearls?"

The formal warning, quite familiar to Mrs. Finch, as to the penalty of an evidential accessory, even if only after the act, could not stem the spate of her mingled cupidity, jealousy and desperate disappointment.

But she took a deep breath, and a deep drink of whisky-and-soda from a side table, before demanding point-blank:

"Just what do all these discoveries amount to in Scotland Yard terms, inspector?" To say chief inspector was beyond her impolite desire to strike.

"So far, seeing only a fraction of the whole as yet," Pointer began tentatively, with undisturbed official sang-froid, "it looks though Mr. Mills might have inserted that advertisement as—"

"Wait a moment!" she interrupted, rapidly turning over some of her papers. "That jeweller said that the imitations were made in Paris; and two days after Arthur bought the two necklaces as his advance wedding present to Violet, Mills went to Paris on business, to realise on some gold shares both for himself and for me. I'm being quite frank with you, you see."

What Pointer saw was a woman who did not know the meaning of the word, but he made no audible comment and she hurried on vindictively:

"Of course it was Mills who inserted those advertisements! Don't you see that?"

"As I said," Pointer replied, "it looks at present as though he might have done so, unless he can show an impeccable alibi covering the time when this Mr. Elwes Morris was at the Cumberland."

Mrs. Finch's eyes narrowed. "Not likely! And I wouldn't say there was no jealousy at the bottom of it, either," she muttered hoarsely, as though to herself. "He used at one time to have a decided weakness for my daughter. But when, about a year ago"—she rubbed an inky finger on her blotting-pad with an air of dark absorption—"I found them secretly confabbing together and taxed them with love-making"—her eyes, as she flashed a glance up at the silently attentive chief inspector, were virtually "spitting fire" as is said of an angry malevolent cat—" they both swore to me that nothing could be farther from either of them. And as it was just about that time that Arthur Walsh and Violet fell passionately in love with each other, why that was that!" Mrs. Finch said with a sweeping gesture and an enigmatic smile.

"But last evening Mills contrived to meet me on my way to town, and almost sobbed—I was too dazed by the news to do so, even if I were of the cry-baby sort!—as he blurted out, without the least consideration for my feelings, as her mother, that Violet had been found by some one in his flat at the Mews, murdered! He said that she must have taken my key and let herself in, or have been let in by some one she had arranged to meet there. And because I thought the dreadful affair awfully hard luck on Mills, as tenant of the flat, while he declared the whole thing—why she had gone there and whom she had met there and why she was murdered—a nightmare mystery to him, as it was to me—and because, too, I own that I didn't want my business partner to get into any such trouble innocently (as I believed, fool and dupe that I was!) just at this juncture in our commercial affairs, I confess that I promised to secure him from it by giving him a sound alibi."

She was obliged to pause for breath after rattling all this off at a rate that would have prevented any word of intervention from the chief inspector, had he been disposed to say any, as he was not. But the pause was so far from being for self-control that she screamed:

"And he was there all the time! Gone to meet her there! Played the part of the rajah's confidential secretary, probably. Violet always was a mug! And of course she had the pearls for him with her! And because she saw through his disguise, though he is a very clever actor, and recognised Mills himself, he killed her. And he's got both those strings of splendid pearls that belong to me now!"

In the silence that momentarily followed, Pointer's first reflection was that Mrs. Finch at any rate made no doubt but that her daughter had raised a loan on the imitation string knowing it to be false, since she had taken the real ones to sell to the advertised purchaser. But he had his own reasons for breaking the silence by saying that "Mr. Walsh believes and Miss Lovelace says she now agrees with him that Miss Finch never suspected that the string she pledged was an imitation one. Mr. Walsh is confident that his wife must have gone to the Mews because she was on the track of the missing string."

"And the newspaper cutting in her bag?" asked Mrs. Finch with recovered coolness, lighting a cigarette and blowing the smoke indifferently in the chief inspector's face.

"Put there by some one else—after she was killed."

Mrs. Finch seemed to consider this possibility. Then she shook her mop of coarse, grey-streaked hair. "Can't see it," she said briefly. "No. Violet and Mills were in the sale of the pearls together. I'll tell you how the thing was worked." She pushed her papers away and cocked one thin knee over the other. "Violet wanted money. She jumped at the chance of selling the pearls and chancing Arthur's not noticing the difference. So she sets Mills to get those perfect imitations made in Paris, while on his business there for me. She tells him to keep his eyes open for any one who would be likely to buy the real ones from her for cash, and take them out of England. A foreigner would be best, she says. Mills thinks it over and sees how he can clear the board for himself. I don't suppose he meant murder, beforehand. Though, as I said, he may have had something like it in for Violet when she fell in love with Arthur Walsh and engaged herself to him. For Mills is a vindictive devil, and as cunning as an old fox.

"Violet herself fixes the meeting with 'the rajah's secretary ' at Mill's flat to keep it safe from me as well as Arthur. And I noticed that Mills was not at all keen on coming down with me. Didn't I tell you that he really left me just a little after three o'clock? He tears back, changes in his car, goes to his flat to meet Vi as the rajah's man, and gets both strings of pearls. For I shouldn't wonder if he'd already bought the smaller one outright.

"But he wouldn't want to lose that money!" Mrs. Finch's greedy eyes were aflame as she cried. "I see what happened about that! He guessed that she had put it in that old cabin trunk where she always kept her private papers and special things, even after she was married. Of course her keys were on her! Catch Violet stirring a step without them!" Something in the tone told of black anger. "That's why he came back after he'd killed her; came here, quietly stepped back after he was shown out, and got that money too!"

Mrs. Finch was not smoking now. Her hand was shaking. She was in a white-hot rage of frustrated, insensate passion. Greed chiefly but not entirely, Pointer thought.

Her words about having "taxed" her daughter and Mills with being in love with each other, meant that she would have opposed it. And something in the eye and tone spoke of jealousy. Real and unalloyed. She was old enough to be Mills's mother, and Pointer fancied that Mrs. Finch was only too well aware of that fact. None the less, he believed her to have been jealous of Mills's affections going elsewhere.

But of one thing he was sure; she was convinced of Mills's guilt. She was not merely pretending to a belief in it. And her story, though frenzied at times, was likely enough, but for the time factor. It was impossible for Mills to have got into Mrs. Walsh's bedroom with the keys taken from her handbag after her death, unlocked the cabin trunk under the bed (however desperately rapid his work) and turned up at Walsh's house at the hour given, if both the times that he specified were correctly stated. About the latter one Pointer thought that there was no doubt. The servant who had let Mills in, and Walsh himself, were independently in perfect agreement as to the hour in question. Incidentally, too, when they traced that telephone call it would be decisive. Yet the maid had been absolutely certain that she had heard Mrs. Walsh move and speak, in her own bedroom, at five o'clock!

Pointer put his doubt to Mrs. Finch. She instantly asked him to touch the bell twice; on which her parlourmaid appeared.

"Look here, Gwendolyn," her mistress said, "I want to get something quite clear about which this officer and I don't agree. He says that Mrs. Walsh didn't leave here yesterday afternoon until after five o'clock. Now isn't that impossible?"

"No, madam, she didn't leave before that," the maid said earnestly. "Five struck just as I heard Mrs. Walsh in her room. I was coming down then for my own tea, from my room. And I tapped on her door to ask if she would like tea. Mrs. Walsh called through the door, 'No, thanks,' and turned on the water, like Miss Vi always used to do when she didn't want to be disturbed, you know, madam."

"Yes, I remember," Mrs. Finch said, frowning thoughtfully. "Well then, Gwendolyn, we'll let that pass. But it was quite half-past five before Mr. Mills turned up, and asked for Mrs. Walsh. That was so, wasn't it?"

"No, madam, it wasn't!" Gwendolyn answered firmly. "It was just quarter-past the hour. We were waiting in the servants' hall for the news from North Ireland. Cook always insists on that. Every day we have to tune-in for North Ireland or there's trouble. Sickening! Mabel and I wanted the B. B. C. Dance Orchestra, which is something like! And just as cook says 'There! That's it!' meaning what she wanted, of course, the front-door bell rang, and it was Mr. Mills, who explained that he'd forgotten his key and wanted to know if Mrs. Walsh was in. Seemed certain she was."

"And you left him waiting in the drawing-room while you inquired," finished her mistress, lighting another cigarette.

"Oh, no, madam! I had no call to. Mr. Mills went away at once," Gwendolyn replied. " He just said 'I can catch her at the Grosvenor Square house,' and ran down the steps again and jumped into his car. I was back in the kitchen the next minute to hear cook still listening to the news from 'the auld counthry,' as she calls it."

"Look here, Gwen," said Mrs. Finch authoritatively, "you've got things mixed. Now don't start to answer back before I'm done! I say you have. Like you did last week when you vowed you hadn't so much as seen the new napkins and then found them in the linen-cupboard. And lots of other times, too. I know you mean to tell the truth, but you're apt to go off half-cocked. Again and again you declare that the gong has gone for dinner before it's been touched."

The maid, who had opened her mouth for a swift retort, shut it with a sheepish grin, contenting herself with an exculpatory: "And half the time it has gone off, madam. As for those serviettes—"

"Now look here," Mrs. Finch cut her short: "It wasn't five yesterday when you spoke through her door to Mrs. Walsh about her tea. It must have been earlier."

But Gwendolyn was not to be shaken on that point. She stuck both obstinately and consistently to her positive statement; and on her own showing it would have been at the time she said, when she was passing down by the bedroom door of the Walshs. And the housemaid was summoned and bore this out again, as she had before.

On which Pointer took her in hand:

"It's a question of exact times; and it's a very important point," he said in his pleasant quiet way. "I'm sure, Mrs. Finch, that Gwendolyn wants to help us, but I'm wondering if she might not have fancied she heard Mrs. Walsh speaking; if she might not have heard just that reply so often before, called through the door, that yesterday Gwendolyn perhaps took it for granted that she heard them again."

Mrs. Finch took out her cigarette and looked at him.

"Well, sir," the housemaid interpolated, with an apologetic smile for it," that's possible, Gwennie often does think she's been called, when she hasn't been, I mean, if it's about the time for it. She's always saying the postman's knocked (that elderly postman who comes of an evening always knocks") —this last in an aside to Mrs. Finch, who paid no attention to it—"when she's waiting for a letter. And I know she's said before now that she heard you come in, madam, and then we've heard you come in later on. Gwennie certainly does think she hears what it's about time for her to hear. I mean—"

She hesitated lamely, and Pointer turned to Gwendolyn herself. He suggested that the voice she had heard speaking through the door was some one imitating Mrs. Walsh's voice. Didn't it sound muffled?—the two words rather blurred? In answer, and looking very excited, Gwendolyn exclaimed:

"Oh, yes, sir, it was like that!" The voice she had heard had had just Miss Violet's—Mrs. Walsh's —way of saying things through the door, " over her shoulder-like, without stopping what she was doing." But Gwendolyn admitted that the words she had heard had sounded indistinctly. And, alter a few further attempts to explain more clearly what she had already made quite clear, the girl was dismissed.

"Sharp of you, chief inspector (but you look as sharp as they make 'em ") Mrs. Finch said when the maids had closed the door, "to spot the probability that it wasn't Violet at all in her bedroom when Gwen thought she heard her. Not Violet, but Mills, eh?" Mrs. Finch said coolly. And Pointer's repulsion was deepened by her unfeeling way of discussing the investigations into the murder of her own daughter. Whatever Violet Finch had been or done . . . could not be wondered at in a child shaped and trained by such a mother.

But having learned what he needed to know, Pointer left the house in his car, picking up Sewell, as arranged, to tell him the facts.

"Then Mrs. Walsh wasn't alive at five o'clock!" Sewell exclaimed after hearing them.

"It's rather that we don't know that she was alive then, than that we have any proof that she was then alive," Pointer said, "though the doctor is inclined to fix the hour when she was killed as about four o'clock."

"And so Mills, after all, has no alibi at all for yesterday afternoon, from three o'clock on! From where he left Mrs. Finch it would take him only an easy three-quarters of an hour's driving to reach the Mews. That would give him ample time to change somewhere on the way into 'Mr. Morris.' He could then be at his flat in that character by four o'clock; let Mrs. Walsh in or be let in by her according to their arrangement; murder her, after getting from her the larger string of pearls; go back to her bedroom for the money he had already paid her for the smaller string, if he had done so; or to get that string also if still in her trunk! But that theory leaves the mysterious telephone call to Walsh unexplained. That extraordinary telephone call quite beats me!" Sewell was all agog.

"Of course I'm professionally out of the case, I'm afraid; since my commission was to clear Mrs. Walsh from any suspicion of having known that those pearls she pledged were imitations. Well! All this hardly points in that direction, does it?"

"It certainly doesn't look, so far, likely that Mrs. Walsh, or Miss Finch as she was then, wasn't up to the neck in the pearls fraud," Pointer said slowly. "But then, it wasn't likely from the first, according to Miss Lovelace's story, as Miss Finch herself endorsed it in writing. And nothing's yet decisively certain, or proved beyond question. I'm now going to see Mr. Walsh. One of us two—you, for choice—had better tell him what we've learned. And, by the way, how did you get on with the bank manager! Was he as helpful as you hoped?"

"He was. What he told me fits in with what you, I fancy, think (and incidentally, what Mrs. Finch thinks, she says) about Mills's purchase outright of the smaller string of pearls." It appeared, Sewell continued, that Mills's bank manager, who had been glad when he closed his account, had said that Mills had had about three thousand pounds in his current account; and had drawn it all out on the day before the Receiving Order against Mrs. Finch was issued, taking it in hundred-pound notes.

"Which he probably changed at various money-changers within the hour, and then changed back again. It would be worth the loss since it would obliterate the trail," Pointer said. "We shall try to trace the notes, of course, but it won't be possible beyond the first change, I fear."

"And now he's probably got in hand pearls valued around three thousand pounds as well," Sewell said musingly. "Just double what he took out of the bank. Well, well! I'm sorry for Arthur Walsh when he learns what we have got to tell him. Though I shall underline the possibility of there eventuating the beatification of his wife when all the facts are discovered and used for her. In common honesty, however, I must hint that there's some doubt of that. But, in common humanity, too, I'll mention it as possible.

"And Kitty won't like the news, either. She's been a staunch supporter of Mrs. Walsh's innocence from the first, you know. And there is this on her side"—Sewell paused to eye Pointer with his face screwed up tightly—"we both feel sure Miss Lovelace knew all about that cutting before we had a cleverly-arranged opportunity to find it. I'll eat my hat if that's not the truth!"

Chapter Fifteen: Marks Of Gilding Are Found On A Cloth

There was a fresh arrangement between the two that Pointer would join Sewell at Friars Halt about an hour later.

Sewell was shown into Colonel Walsh's study, where he found the Colonel pacing the hearth. Usually the most courteous of men, he gave Sewell the briefest of welcomes before, coming to a stop in face of his visitor and looking at him fixedly, he said, "Arthur went to you as to a sort of diviner, seer, and so on, didn't he? Well, what do you divine or see, eh?"

"Nothing of the former, sir, and thick fog as to the latter," Sewell replied frankly.

The Colonel snorted, his head held high, his restless gaze roaming the gardens through the windows. " 'Fog,' eh? I find it clear enough! That unfortunate son of mine, Sewell, married a thorough wrong 'un; and in my humble opinion he's well out of it, bad as was the way of his unexpected and madly-resented release. That duping of Ann Lovelace's kind heart—well, could anything be more dastardly?"

Sewell held his own head no less high, however, as he replied, "But, sir, there are two ways of regarding that."

"The way of common sense and the way of its absence!" snorted the Colonel. "Of course, if you insist, as Arthur does, that if a black thing's shiny, that proves it's really white, I have nothing to say."

"You mean, sir, that you take Miss Lovelace's first view of that pearl transaction?" Sewell asked with an accent of incredulity.

"Ann Lovelace's first view was the only intelligent view," the Colonel barked with a grimace as though he smelled bad fish. "And I say that, whatever caused her death, Arthur's a lucky man to be rid of a wife like that. Of course, this is confidential, Sewell! But it's as plain as is the nose on my face."

Sewell's only response was to say, "About those pledged pearls, I should tell you that it may possibly be proved that Miss Finch, as Mrs. Walsh was then, had no idea they were expert imitations."

The Colonel listened with an expression that said, "You poor dupe!" as clearly as words could have said it. But "Indeed?" was his verbal synonym.

"If some still unsuspected person had stolen the real string and deftly substituted a prepared copy, Miss Finch might not have dreamt of either possibility," Sewell ploughed on-sturdily.

"You haven't seen Arthur just lately, I believe," the Colonel said without arguing the other's last postulate. "He's dreadfully upset. But I think and hope that even he begins to see daylight. Dimly, perhaps, as yet. And, poor chap, he tries to shut his eyes to it. But he's found out about the money."

"What money?" Sewell asked blankly.

"The money his fiancee banked from the sale of the string she borrowed on," the Colonel replied grimly. "She had five pounds-odd in her bank balance a fortnight before the wedding, and one thousand and five pounds-odd exactly a week before it. And the money was paid into her account in hundred-pound notes. That smaller string cost just that, Arthur admits. Just the thousand!"

"How does he himself explain it?" Sewell asked with intense curiosity and much real feeling.

"Oh, he babbles about 'lucky at cards,' 'little scoops at gaming tables' . . . where she lost four hundred one night she might have won a thousand another night . . . that sort of stuff! But in his secret heart he must suspect the truth. No, it came from the sale of the smaller string of pearls all right, Sewell. And, even so, mind you, she didn't offer to refund to Ann Lovelace her loaned four hundred pounds. She let Arthur pay that for her without a whisper of this new money of her own in the bank."

It was a facer. "I suppose the manager let Arthur know about it?" Sewell asked slowly.

"Yes, Ann thoughtfully suggested that, as Violet, when she had borrowed the money, had spoken ruefully of having only a few pounds left in her bank balance, it would be a pretty idea to bestow it on some charity in Violet's name. She advised Arthur, for that purpose, to ascertain the exact amount standing to the credit of Violet. He did so, poor fellow, and received this reply. I was in the room when it came; so was Ann. He looked as though something had hit him hard. No wonder! Something had.

"His first doubt of his adored Violet's innocence. Ann finally got out of him what the trouble was. Women are clever at such things. But here he comes! I'm off! I try not to see him, poor lad, until his senses have somewhat recovered from that stab." Unlatching the window and stepping through it, the Colonel extended his long legs to a quick march. And Sewell had an idea that the father cheered himself on with hope of a marriage much more to his liking for his son, and was therefore, on the whole, inclined to think that the murder of Violet Walsh had simplified things.

As for Arthur, when he hurried in, his hair was wild, his tie was askew, and he almost barged into Sewell before he seemed to see him at all.

"I wanted a word with my father," he murmured in excuse. "The fact is, Sewell, there's some foul conspiracy being worked up against my poor murdered Violet! Worked up by some devil, Sewell! And you seem just as powerless as the rest of us to discover him! Some one's damnably clever—damnably!" He broke off in choking tones and started after his father, but Sewell stopped him with a persuasive hand on his arm.

"Look here, what's happened? Tell me what's happened, Walsh?" he urged.

For a moment Arthur stood silent. Then he faced his confidential and chosen investigator squarely, eye to eye, as he answered: "I asked the manager of my wife's bank to let me know the exact amount of the small sum her death left standing as her balance. I got a letter, this morning, informing me officially that a thousand pounds had been paid in to her credit some fourteen days ago. Of course, I took the car up and asked to see the manager himself. The information was correct. Bank notes to the total of a thousand pounds were paid in to her account in one-hundred pound notes—by a lady—shortly before closing time, before three o'clock on the date specified.

"The writing on the paying-in slip looks like Violet's, of course. Shown her photograph, the receiving clerk recognised it as that of the lady who had handed him the money. . . ." Arthur's voice stopped for a full moment on this. "Now, either it was Violet—and that money wasn't hers at all, but just banked by her for some other person for whom it was definitely intended—or else it was some one cleverly made-up to resemble her closely, some one wearing her clothes, or much more likely clothes that were a copy of hers.

"My father, of course, obstinately refuses to see this, but Ann quite agrees with me. So does Kitty. Personally, I incline to the idea that some one induced Violet to bank the thousand pounds in her own name, as a great favour, and gave some quite plausible reason for the request, and for the absolute secrecy she wanted, or he wanted, kept about the favour. And if Violet promised that, Sewell, nothing and no one could have got a word of its betrayal out of her. She was as straight as . . ."

"As your father declares Miss Lovelace is," Sewell finished rather maliciously.

"As Ann is," Arthur said heartily. "She's a brick, too, Sewell! I never thought Ann Lovelace could be so true a friend as she's shown herself to me, these days. And as she is now remorsefully showing herself to my wife's memory. She was completely bowled over when I confided to her what was in the letter from Violet's bank. For she had characteristically insisted on sharing the bad news in it—as she had seen that it must be to account for its effect on me."

"Umph-umph," murmured Sewell with more significance than sympathy. "Quite! Quite!"

"But, like me," Arthur exulted, "Ann saw what must be the true explanation at once. It takes a good woman to do justice to a good woman's character."

"Miss Kitty Walsh also has shown herself a staunch friend," responded Sewell.

"She has, indeed," was the instant rejoinder. "But, then, Kitty—"Arthur paused. "She's an angel, is Kitty," he resumed. "While, of course Ann Lovelace is a woman of the world to her fingertips. That means, she isn't swayed by her heart only, but by her head even more. Ann's convinced of Violet's absolute innocence in that pearl pledge, because she realises more and more how certainly Violet had the kind of nature that could easily be duped." Arthur fixed Sewell's questioning eyes with haggard eyes of defence. "Truthful, honourable, loyal. ... I don't believe Violet could ever suspect evil in any one around her. She trusted others as she confidently expected to be trusted herself."

Sewell felt urgent need of some refreshment. His head felt thick, almost dazed by conflicting thoughts. Passing through the hall, he and Arthur found Pointer being taken to the library, and the three men went in together.

"I haven't told Walsh anything of our activities yet," Sewell said promptly. "I've been hearing many things instead." Here he turned meaningly to Arthur, who very gruffly and briefly passed on the new facts about Violet's bank balance. Pointer did not, at the moment, add to the speaker's evident distress by questioning him on the subject, only asking for a memorandum of the original balance, and the date when this had been increased by the said thousand pounds. But presently, as Arthur's composure was somewhat regained—after motioning him to a seat where eavesdropping would have no opportunity—the chief inspector mentioned that there seemed a possibility that it might not, in reality, have been Mrs. Walsh whom the parlourmaid had heard moving about and speaking like Mrs. Walsh, in the latter's own bedroom, at the hour fairly proved to have been five o'clock, adding the corroborative opinion of the doctor, who was decidedly inclined to put the hour of the murdered wife's death as "not later than four o'clock," although he had of course deferred to what had seemed like indisputable evidence to the contrary.

As if unable to contain himself longer on hearing these startlingly poignant possibilities, Arthur jumped convulsively out of his chair, pacing agitatedly to and fro as he exclaimed with clenched hands and blazing eyes, "As I said to Sewell, there's been some damnable crime against my unsuspecting, innocent Violet! Those cursed pearls I gave her were at the bottom of it, I'm afraid. But not the whole of it! Some well-concocted story was told to my poor girl to get her to keep silent about that thousand pounds she was holding for somebody. ..."

"I wonder if the smaller string of pearls were stolen to fit that amount," Sewell broke in unexpectedly. "I mean by some one who knew that exactly that amount had just been paid in to her own credit by Mrs. Walsh at her bank."

"Do you suspect who the criminal is?" Arthur savagely demanded of Pointer, facing him, hands thrust into his pockets fiercely, feet well apart, chin thrust forward aggressively.

"Certain things seem to implicate Mr. Mills," Pointer began in his characteristically calm way, but was interrupted by the almost maniacal cry:

"Mills! By God! the devil came to me red-handed from her murder, after searching her things at Ennismore Gardens!" A slight froth showed on his writhing lips. "No wonder he didn't want to go back to his flat! But I insisted on his coming with Kitty and me to see for himself that the phoned message was a hoax. It was well for him that I thought so then. I'll never, never forgive myself for that! But. . . ."

But before his choking voice could continue, the door opened and Kitty Walsh entered. Pointer, if not Sewell, was very sorry to see her at that tense moment. But she came at his own request for a fresh going over of her memories, and he could not, therefore, ask her to postpone the interview.

He went through yesterday very carefully with her, and Kitty did her best to recollect each incident, however small, after she had met Mills at Grosvenor Square, until she remembered the room swinging round her as she saw Violet's head. She was foggy after that. The next thing she remembered at all was putting down a glass of water which some one had first held to her lips and then put into her hand. She was sitting up by that time, on a chair by the door—with her back to the fireplace—she added with a shudder. She remembered putting down the glass of water and spilling most of it—it was very full—and then Mr. Cook helped her up on to her feet and down the stairs to the open front door. After that Kitty's recollections, she said, could add nothing more, and certainly nothing to what the three men already knew. Pointer acquiesced, but nevertheless put one more incidental question, namely: "Can you remember the colour of the tablecloth on the little table you recollect spilling the glass of water on?" But, although Kitty willingly searched her mind back to the incident of the water spilled weakly on the table, she could not remember about the cloth on it, except vaguely that she had felt one there.

But at this point in the reconstruction Arthur broke in with excited eagerness to assist in even so seemingly trivial a detail: "Sewell! I remember that little tablecover perfectly! It was a square thing, about the size of a large table-napkin, I should say, with bright red-and-blue checks on it. And, by Jove," he ejaculated with mounting heat as if there might be some inexplicable clue in the point, "if you look at your police photographs of the room, chief inspector, you won't find any cloth whatever on that little table by the window, but you'll see the ash tray still on it that stood in the centre of the red-and-blue checked square when Kitty and Mills and I entered the room. Its crude colours caught one's eyes before any of us saw the body of my Violet."

Pointer nodded. "No cloth. Just the tray," he confirmed.

"Then how in the world did you know that there had been a tablecloth on it at all?" Kitty asked him in a tone of absolute awe at such second sight. But Pointer only looked mysteriously wise; and Arthur broke in again.

The absorbing interest for him lay in the fact, not in the detective certainty or lucky guess, of the chief inspector, and his voice was shrill as he exclaimed:

"Then in that brief moment of my going to telephone to the police"—the telephone was in the hall, they all knew—" Mills must have switched away the cloth, replacing the tray carefully on the table, and stuffed it heaven knows where! Inside his coat, possibly, though it was by no means a mere pocket-handkerchief."

"There is such a table-square as you describe, sir, in a drawer of the kitchen dresser in the basement," Pointer said slowly.

"But what on earth could be Mills' reason?" Arthur asked, as though of the Heaven above him.

"One explanation might be that there was some mark or stain on it that Mr. Mills didn't want noticed. . . ." And the chief inspector fell silent, his eyes on his shoe-tips.

"When is he to be arrested?" Arthur asked thickly.

"He has been requested to come to my rooms at the Yard in two hours' time from now. And if he cannot or does not give a satisfactory explanation of everything he will be detained while further investigations are being made."

"Detained! You mean arrested? Hung?" Arthur cried with leaping eyeballs.

"Arrested, quite possibly, Mr. Walsh. Hanging. I am thankful to say, lies with jury and judge. But, by the way, I asked you to think very carefully over that strange telephone summons you received. Has nothing explanatory occurred to you in connection with it, sir?"

"Nothing, chief inspector. Absolutely nothing that could shed the faintest ray of light on that weird message." And of this whole terrible mystery that most tragically-appropriate yet quite misunderstood summons seems the most expressive silence of common cogitations until Arthur drove away gloomily, after receiving a nod from each of the others in response to his parting request to be "kept posted."

"How in the world, chief inspector, could even your wits know about that absent cover on the little occasional table?" Sewell exclaimed with keen curiosity when they were again en route in the car.

"Miss Kitty Walsh told us, you remember, that in her still faint condition she upset almost a tumblerful of water over the top of that table," Pointer answered conclusively, and seemed to think that he had given a complete explanation of his knowledge. But not so Sewell, who asked, with friendly exasperation: "Well? What of it?" Only to be countered with the question:

"What became of all that water?" With the quizzical rider: "It's my particular business, you know, to see that nothing gets lost in a case."

Sewell laughed. "You mean that the top of the little table wasn't noticeably wet, only a few minutes later?"

"I mean, on the contrary," Pointer said significantly, "that—having put down some papers on it, when entering a note on one of them—I had especially seen to it that the table top was perfectly dry. And as the most impassioned tidiness would not have stopped to dry it at such a time, it is obvious that the water must have been absorbed by a tablecloth of some sort which was no longer there, had been evidently taken away so scrupulously as to replace the ash-tray without it."

"Bloodstained, somehow, of course," Sewell said sapiently, but without his usual shrewd judgment.

"And the Yard's men wouldn't have noted and listed that?" Pointer commented sceptically. Adding what aroused the other's detective interest afresh: "Nor would bloodstains on it have mattered unless actual fingerprints."

Sewell felt himself swimming in deep waters and a little out of his depth with this man's wide-sweeping intelligence, until Pointer continued: "Since there was so much blood about in the room, spots on the little tablecloth wouldn't have meant any added danger, unless they were actual fingerprints in blood. And that there could have been not the least vestige of, or they would have been listed when the cloth was seen in the kitchen drawer.

"But if not bloodprints," Pointer, as a rare token of profound concentration debated aloud with himself, "what could there have been about that little tablecloth which Mills—if it was Mills, as I think—knew must point to him? Just as the original bits of paper undoubtedly did."

"Eh???" came in almost a screech from the rapt Sewell.

"Or 'probably' did," Pointer conscientiously amended. "From the first, that seemed their only explanation. Though why he strewed them where we found them does beat me as yet, I confess. But that carefully-removed tablecloth? No fingerprints of any kind were on it, I know for certain. Inspector Watts examined that cloth himself. Of course, I shall look it over, too, if it is still in existence. By my instructions nothing has been sent to the laundry from the house. But—what—?" The chief inspector stared straight ahead of him as a red signal pulled his car up.

"Even you, surely, chief inspector, can't possibly hope to guess what it could have been?" Sewell gasped, with the zest of a boy.

Pointer's eyelids narrowed to the glittering slit of a chamois hunter searching the distance for his prey as he said resolutely, "We both believe that Mr. Mills was alone in that room where Mrs. Walsh —your client, as it were— was killed. Then follow him, Sewell, in your mind, as I am following him in mine. Nothing there, that we know of, to mark him, except blood; and I'm not looking for blood. The fire is electric. Nothing wet. Besides water wouldn't give anything away. No! If there is a clue to him on that little tablecloth he put it there on returning to the room with Mr. Walsh and Miss Kitty Walsh! He may have grasped the little table on which it lay; perhaps as Mr. Walsh sprang to the body of his murdered wife. And by that clutch he left—I think—some smear or mark, which linked the cloth with—what? With himself? How could it? Mr. Mills follows no pursuit or trade that carries its stamp.

"Then did it link up in some way with where he had been? Now, take the trail afresh with me, Sewell, and follow him leaving the place. He slipped down the stairs; nothing there. And out through the front door; nothing there. Besides, even if there had been seas of fresh paint, he would have a perfect right to fresh paint on his hands from his own front door, seeing that he passed through it again with Miss Kitty Walsh and Mr. Walsh when he went back with them.

"No, it's something linking the tablecloth, the room, with some place with which it must on no account be linked! His office? But anything linking them with himself, or his own place, would pass without question, just as his ordinary fingerprints would and did.

"I can only think of one spot with which Mr. Mills wouldn't want his flat linked—and that spot was Mrs.

Walsh's bedroom, the bedroom that he searched, we think, on his way from his flat to Mr. Walsh's own house. Now was there anything there that might leave such a stain or token on his left hand that, when he pulled off his gloves in his flat, might mark that little tablecloth—if he took hold of it—and leave traces of something only to be found in Mrs. Walsh's bedroom? Powder? Scent? But she was killed in his flat! So anything of hers found there would not be remarkable, could be explained, one would think. . . ."

Suddenly Pointer's eyes gleamed. He had seen his chamois. "The radiator! Did you notice the radiator by the door of her bedroom, Sewell? No? Well, it was still quite tacky with fresh gilding yesterday. It had been a forgotten order, when this room was got ready for the Walshs; and the fresh gilding was hastily done the very day of their arrival, Mabel told me. There is a wall recess just there, and the tackiness, therefore, was not likely to be noticed. But let any of that gilding get on to the tablecloth in Mr. Mills' flat, and—since there was no touch of it on the murdered bride herself —it would be exceedingly difficult to account for its presence there.

"Yes, it could be gilding, unconsciously adhering to Mr. Mills' hand and betrayingly impressed on the little tablecloth in his flat if he had chanced to unluckily transfer it by taking hold of the cloth, for any reason, with a feverishly-hot pressure. It could be just that!"

The chief inspector drove his now speechlessly-admiring professional disciple hurriedly to the Mews, where both men had the delight of finding the decisive evidence almost uncannily testifying to Pointer's genius for detective reasoning. For the little tablecloth which Arthur had accurately remembered was still guarded in the locked kitchen drawer at the Mews, and on it was a conspicuously incongruous but quite immovable splotch of the same fresh gilding as was on the radiator in what had been the bedroom of Violet Walsh.

"And now," Pointer said quietly to Sewell, carefully enclosing his trophy in a sealed, labelled and duly witnessed large envelope, "we reach the vital core of this evidence: namely, how and why Mr. Mills got that identical gilding on his hand. To me it seems obvious that, in his frightful haste, he must have let something fall behind that re-gilt radiator, the tackiness of which his excitement did not let him notice while his hand frantically sought the dropped object behind or under it."

CHAPTER SIXTEEN: ANOTHER POSSIBLE MOTIVE IS DISCOVERED

"Could it be a pearl which broke off and rolled under the radiator?" Sewell suggested when they were off again for Ennismore Gardens. But the chief inspector reminded him that Mr. Walsh had had the pearls all freshly restrung for his wedding gift, although it was, of course, quite possible that the smaller string had been caught on something and too hastily jerked free. . . .

Pointer had telephoned from outside the garage to the Yard for a detective-mechanic; and one was waiting for them at the house.

Mrs. Finch was out. So was Arthur. The three men went up together to the bedroom. Again its door was unlocked and re-locked behind them, and in a brief time the mechanic had the radiator out into the room.

Nothing was to be seen behind it, Sewell thought in great disappointment. But Pointer discovered, on an elbow formed by the bend of the feeding-pipe, a little gold ring that looked, to less keenly-searching eyes, like a bit of the gilding. It was unmistakably a wedding-ring.

Nothing else rewarded a thorough hunt, and the radiator was accordingly returned and fixed in its recess, the mechanic departing as soon as that was done. The little 22-carat gold circle was then closely examined. But there was no inscription in it, no date.

"Mrs. Walsh is the only woman connected with the case, so far, whose finger it would fit," Pointer felt sure. "Her wedding-ring is at the Yard." He tagged this one securely, and the mechanic had carried a message from Pointer to another of the Yard's men.

"Could she have been married before? To Mills, do you think, chief inspector?" Sewell gasped. "And was Mrs.

Finch right—that mad jealousy as well as the pearls was the motive? Or was it just a week-end ring?" he debated alternatively.

"I don't believe that Mr. Mills would have tried to get it out again if it had been only that last," Pointer replied. "He was in great danger of being found here, or seen coming out of this room. Under the circumstances, I don't think he would have hunted for it at all unless it had been, or seemed to be, of vital importance to him.

"This ring suggests that the cabin-trunk under the bed may have contained—" Pointer's voice fell away into the silence of profound thought; but Sewell made an imploring gesture, and he responded: "I think it might have been a wedding-certificate that took Mr. Mills here—quite apart from any question of the pearls," he finished. "And I am sending a reliable man to search the registers for a possible previous marriage of Violet Finch's."

"That Mills felt that he must secure that ring," Sewell said, "is proof enough that he was her murderer—absolute proof, I say. Who else but the murderer would have known that her things would be searched, and that the discovery of this ring would follow unless he recovered it first? That it would point directly to him and his motive, his additional motive? For undoubtedly there was raging jealousy there, as well as greed. If there was a marriage, was it in her own name? I wonder, and was it legally dissolved?" he speculated on. "By jove, this is a 'volte face,' and one that will break Arthur Walsh's heart, poor fellow!"

"But not his father's heart," Pointer said.

"Rather not! Colonel Walsh'll burn a special row of candles to his patron saint," Sewell replied with a smile, adding dolefully, as he saw Pointer getting into his official car: "This is where the amateur gets bumped off, chief inspector. Oh, I know that I'm dining with you to-night; but I've got to live unsatisfied till then, worse luck!"

"I'll let you know if anything of importance turns up," Pointer answered consolingly; "but I don't think it will. One of my men will start at once to hunt through the registers at Somerset House, and I must hurry back for an appointment with Mr. Mills."

At the Yard, the discovered ring was found to be exactly the same size as the one taken from Violet Walsh's dead hand. Pointer had felt sure that it would prove so, after his first look at it; and he locked both away as Mr. Mills was announced.

He was immediately ushered in, looking quite calm and unruffled. But at the chief inspector's opening the interview with the obligatory warning, Mills' lips blanched. Not so his sunburned cheeks, however. Pointer had suspected their deep tan at sight. To the warning Mills offered no real protest—although he seemed astonished by it. And the chief inspector passed at once to an outline of the case that Mills would have to face. He began it with Mills' surreptitious visit to the Walsh's bedroom before his open return to the house when he rang at the front door and next went on to Grosvenor Square. The official recapitulation finished with the fact that Mills was confidently believed to be the man who had played the part of the hypothetical Rajah's "secretary," after inserting the advertisements under that head.

Mills denied everything. The sweat was standing on his face in grotesquely brown beads. He wiped it away at once, but instantly stuffed the handkerchief with which he did it into his pocket. After that he preferred to suffer the discomfort, rather than the greater embarrassment, and let the oddly swart drops trickle where they would, winking them out of his eyes. Pointer did not tell him of the finding of the wedding-ring, with its allied facts and sinister implications. They were kept in reserve for the moment.

"You're all mixed up, chief inspector," Mills finally declared with an effort at bravado. "All this story about the pearls and the advertisements—" But Pointer stayed these hollow protests with stiff questions as to dates and hours when "Elwes Morris" was known to have been at one or other of the two hotels. And here Mills came off very badly. He blustered about having purposely avoided people because of the financial trouble in which he and his partner, Mrs. Finch, were involved; but he was unable to clear himself in respect of any of the specific points which Pointer took him over very carefully because of their importance to the issue, and he was consequently told that he would be detained pending further inquiries about the pearl necklaces.

At this Mills shouted, "What for? What for?" in a sort of frenzy. "You know that there was another man in my rooms that day! You can't deny that, no matter how you try. The man who telephoned to Walsh while I was at Grosvenor Square. His wife was alive then, at five-thirty—if that's what your talk of 'the pearl necklaces' means!"

"That conclusion doesn't necessarily follow, Mr. Mills," Pointer said coldly. "But you are not detained on a charge of murder."

Mills said no more. And he was conducted from the room with despair in his eyes.

Pointer sat on fixedly, looking straight ahead of him as he pondered—

That strange message . . .! And 'Father Walsh' still in his religious Retreat . . .! It was sent at half-past five. . . . If Pointer's theory was right, Violet was murdered by the time it reached Arthur Walsh. Then why was it sent? Was it possible that the secret search in Violet's room was done at her own instigation . . .? That she was selling her pearls to the Rajah "secretary," Pointer thought might be taken as a fact. . . .

Here his coiling and uncoiling debate was actively interrupted. His man entered. He had found the record of a marriage in a registry office, some fourteen months ago, "between Violet Finch, spinster, of Ennismore Gardens, and Herbert Mills, bachelor, of Green Street Court, Mayfair." The witnesses had evidently been provided by the Registry Office in question.

So the murdered bride was really not Walsh's wife at all! But at her death still the undivorced wife of Mills! This amazing and fundamentally prime news was phoned to Sewell in their arranged code, and he lost no time in speeding to the chief inspector and eagerly accepting his invitation to accompany him on his proposed interview with Mrs. Finch—or Mrs. Gray, to give her the rightful title consistently ignored by herself and every one else.

The interview was indeed cyclonic when Mrs. Finch was told the unquestionable facts just ascertained. The news—if it was really unsuspected news—that her murdered daughter had died as the wife of the impecunious Mills and not as that of the wealthy and wealth-inheriting heir, Arthur Walsh, sent the unbridled woman into so extraordinarily violent a rage as to make Pointer eye her speculatively, to Sewell's keenly interested observation.

Mrs. Finch, in her uncontrollable fury, raged and looked as though she herself would willingly have torn Violet limb from limb had she been still alive. What was more, from the chief inspector's concerned point of view, she hurled to his adroitly probing questions some furious replies which for the first time revealed the variously gravid circumstances that she had not only induced Arthur to settle five thousand a year on Violet, but had also wrung from the latter, privately, a legally executed document endowing her mother absolutely with one thousand a year from the date of her daughter's marriage to Arthur. While at the same time Arthur had signed a will leaving everything he possessed, or was entitled at the time of his death, to Violet absolutely—should he predecease her and there be no offspring of their marriage.

Learning these facts and seeing that evil face, Sewell began to share the Colonel's belief that Violet Finch's death had really been a blessing for Arthur Walsh. Now, however, even that consolation was enlarged, for Violet had never been his wife—the settlements were null and void . . .! Pointer, too, privately thought that Mrs. Finch would have delighted to hang Mills with her own hands. "Just as well he's in safe keeping!" Sewell said as they left the woman figuratively, if not also literally, foaming at the mouth. "She'd have his eyes out, at least, otherwise."

"Yes," Pointer agreed meditatively. "Odd!"

"Why 'odd?' She looks 'capable de tout.'"

"The way she takes it is odd, none the less," Pointer said. "As though she herself had been sold, somehow."

"The wedding was quite a gala affair, but I understand from the solicitors that it was Violet who had to sign for everything," Sewell said with a grin. Then he looked up to add: "You know, I'm somehow convinced that Miss Kitty Walsh feels certain that Ann Lovelace is a hostile element.   That's in confidence, of course. But where does she come in?"

"Miss Walsh is rather prejudiced against Miss Lovelace," Pointer replied absent-mindedly. "We know she strongly sided with the supposed Miss Finch," he added; "and I'm afraid she backed the wrong horse there. Though possibly Miss Lovelace meant to and did lay a trap for the supposed Miss Finch over that loan on the accepted pearls as security."

"You mean she knew they were imitation? You think both young women knew it, and that each believed she was besting the other?" Sewell persisted.

Pointer nodded. "Looks rather like it. Miss Lovelace has some very fine pearls of her own, I'm told. I think she may have hoped to do just what she did do: go to Mr. Walsh with the proof of his fiancee's dishonesty."

"And he, poor chap, nearly knocked her down for daring to cast a doubt on his adored Violet." Sewell's tone changed eloquently as he concluded with keen interest: "I wonder what Arthur Walsh will say about it."

So did Pointer privately. And the other resumed: "The Colonel was not far off the mark, though too sweeping altogether, in declaring that 'a liar is always a trickster.' I wonder if the pseudo Mrs. Walsh cared for Mills all the time in her heart of hearts? And yet, you know, she seemed to me just a lively, frank, rattle-brain—too completely unsophisticated to hide a thought."

But Pointer was obliged to drop Sewell and his reflections, at this point, and hurry back to the Yard. He found nothing new there, however, except a confirmation of Mr. Gray's alibi for every day except yesterday—the one day that mattered. Yesterday he had driven from Manchester up to Town in the morning, had lunched some business men at the Holborn Grill-room; but he had just strained his wrist, he told Pointer's man, and had driven out to Richmond after lunch to see a doctor friend of his, but Gray had found the sprain so much lighter than he had feared that, tired with his drive up to Town in a troublesome car, instead of troubling his friend, he had had a good sleep in a quiet corner of the Park, driven back to Town, found his wrist hurting afresh, left his car at a garage in Euston Road, at a little before six o'clock, and gone back to Manchester by the six-ten train. The only confirmation obtainable, therefore, was for the hours that were not suspect at all. He had lunched where and when he said, left his car where and when he said, and as he had not taken a ticket, but had paid in the train, it could be proved that he had returned to Manchester at the time that he said that he had. All the rest hung on his own assertions.

Pointer sent in this report to be duly filed, and ordered a swift car. He wanted to get down to Friars Halt at once for a crucial interview with Mr. Walsh.

At its opening, Arthur began a half-hearted assertion that Violet had been cleverly impersonated. But after that one interpolation he listened in a tense silence till the chief inspector had finished. And then he literally raged. For a while he was like a madman, laughing insanely, great roars of laughter that rang through the house.

His father hurried in to ask what was going on.

"Ask him!" Arthur ejaculated, indicating Pointer. "Good God, Pater, what a priceless dupe I've been!' My fiancee!' 'My wife!' There never was such a person!" And again came a burst of wild laughter as he left the two others alone, slamming the door behind him as it assuredly had never been slammed since it was first hung on its stout hinges.

Pointer quietly explained all the amazing facts about Violet Finch's secret marriage to Mr. Mills. The Colonel did not hide his heartfelt joy at the authentic news that he and his were free from any legal connection with "the detestable Finches," alive or dead, before going upstairs for a private word with Arthur. Pointer waited, in case Mr. Walsh should want to see him again.

But the Colonel came back alone. He did not tell the chief inspector that his son lay actually sobbing on his bed. Contenting himself with the message that the latter felt quite unable to continue so painful an interview at the moment. Adding: "But at any rate he's cured. The savants are quite right who say that 'love is a disease.' Love like that my unhappy son lavished on that creature certainly was more an infatuation than normal falling in love. He's all broken up by it. And no wonder! Even my niece, Kitty, will find it, I fear, a great shock. She really liked her!"

"Miss Lovelace, too, seemed quite won over, sir, to the same attitude," Pointer replied.

On which Colonel Walsh shrugged his shoulders with a slight smile, as he observed judicially: "I think that was perhaps carrying noblesse oblige rather too far. Ann, I imagine, was so afraid of being not only unsympathetic to my son, but unjust to his idol, that she was swept over to the warmth of a partisan. But in her heart she never lost, I think, the same innate aversion to the daughter of the notorious 'Mrs. Finch' that I openly felt. And which Arthur must feel now, chief inspector. For no one can now, surely, do more than shudderingly pity the tragic opening-up of the secret history of the murderer's victim. I suppose it was some jealous quarrel with her and her actual husband?

"Or was it more likely for the pearls? My son maintains that she must have bribed Mills to keep silent with one of the strings. I suppose that's quite possible. Anyway, it's a most creditable and clever piece of work on your part, chief inspector," the army man said warmly, "to have unearthed the truth and arrested the murderer within four-and-twenty hours of the murder. A brilliant achievement!"

"Mr. Mills isn't under arrest, sir," Pointer corrected. "And unless we can get more incontestable evidence of guilt, the Public Prosecutor would not sanction such an extreme step."

"You mean that he may still slip out of your net?" The Colonel, who was not a vindictive man, looked rather relieved as he acknowledged: "I can never really approve, in my own mind, chief inspector, of any man swinging for an utterly worthless woman's removal," he owned confidentially.

Pointer did not care to argue this extremely dangerous public question, although his own convictions, based on long professional experience were that an unhung murderer will murder again to satisfy his own particular passion of the moment—whether revenge or jealousy or mere greed. And just then Arthur Walsh came back to join his father and Pointer, looking a physical wreck from shock and sorrow. Sewell, too, was ushered in at the same moment.

He held out his hand to Arthur, nodding to the other two in the room, saying simply to his friend and quondam employer for the murdered woman's defence: "I can't tell you how sorry I am . . ." he began.

Arthur gripped his hand hard, with a muttered, "It's all over, Sewell! Finished!" And then, with a gleam of his previous wildness, he fairly shouted, "I never want to hear her name again! She cheated me from start to finish; poor fool and tool that she made of me!"

"But what about the missing pearls, Walsh?" his friend said questioningly.

"Oh, of course I want them found! Stolen booty that they were!" Arthur said with energy. "The murderer was in the plot, and rounded on his partner—evidently. You must recover them for me at whatever cost, my dear fellow."

Sewell looked beyond him as he answered firmly: "Sorry, but of course, as I take none but purely defensive commissions, you know, I can't take that one."

"You mean you won't aid me to recover those two extremely valuable necklaces, given only as a wedding gift?" Arthur exclaimed in a really scandalised as well as wounded tone.

"Professionally speaking, no," Sewell answered flatly. "But I confess I should like to know what follows, Walsh. For instance, I keenly want to understand that strange telephone message to you," he said.

"So do I!" came emphatically from Arthur; and Colonel Walsh echoed him.

They all three looked inquiringly at Pointer who had picked up a book and was standing turning its pages. He laid it down. "It's by Superintendent Hatherly," he said apologetically. "Quite a textbook on the ruses used by some of the cleverer criminals. But about that telephone message, Mr. Walsh. The Reverend Father Walsh is still out of laymen's reach at all events, in his religious Retreat. Yet the call just mentioned has been definitely traced to him. Otherwise, of course, Mr. Mills would seem the most likely sender."

"Ambrose never sent it," Arthur said decisively. "There's some error in that identification. The man or woman who did send it—must have been an accomplice. Mills was upstairs in the drawing-room; and as yet there's only one telephone in the Grosvenor Square house. So that lets Mills out—"

"He was in the drawing-room?" Pointer asked with surprised emphasis. "Mr. Mills said that he was in the library; and when I repeated that statement to you, Mr. Walsh, you did not correct it."

"I suppose I was thinking of something else. God knows I had horrors enough to occupy my mind!" Arthur replied with savage brusqueness. "At least, they seemed like horrors to me at the time. But what iota of difference to Scotland Yard can it make to know in which particular room he was? He was in the house, and so where he couldn't have used the telephone. Surely the only detail of importance."

The Colonel cocked his eye inquiringly at the chief inspector, who was looking at Arthur as though he were decidedly interested by what he had just learnt.

"It might make all the difference in the world, Mr. Walsh," Pointer observed. "There's a telephone extension in the drawing-room at Grosvenor Square, but none in the library, if I'm right?"

"Quite right. But, again, chief inspector, what difference does that make?"

"Did the Exchange ask you what number you wanted?"

"Yes, but not until I had been given that message."

Pointer's eyes went to the corner.

"Yes, that's a telephone," Colonel Walsh said, keenly on the alert. "And here, just as in the Grosvenor Square house, there are extensions to the drawing-rooms upstairs, and to the bedrooms above that again."

"Then I'll show you gentlemen how that message could have been sent."

Pointer stepped to the corner. In a trice the Colonel showed him the instrument. Pointer lifted it and called up the Yard, to which he sent a code message. Then he put down the receiver.

"Now, if I may, I'll go upstairs to the extension in the drawing-room. And I want you, Mr. Walsh, to answer the phone when it rings. It will be a call from the Yard, yet you'll hear the same message that you heard once before, the one that has puzzled us, only this time it'll be repeated in my voice. For, unlike Mr. Mills, I shall not try and disguise it by a foreign accent."

Pointer was shown upstairs. A moment later the telephone rang. Arthur answered it in record time. And he heard, to his amazement, the voice of the chief inspector speaking, and giving word for word the message which had so startled him before. And as then it was followed by the voice of the Exchange asking what number he wanted. Arthur was too puzzled to reply.

"Hang up," came again in Pointer's voice, and Arthur did so.

Another moment and Pointer was back in the room.

"How's it done?" Arthur asked in sheer stupefaction.

"If the telephone rings," Pointer explained, "and some one in the room where there is an extension takes off the receiver at the same instant as you do down here, then, should you by any chance be disconnected at the Exchange, and if that some one speaks through at once, his words would reach you as though it were spoken by the person who had rung up. I fancy Mr. Ambrose Walsh was disconnected before he spoke one word. That would be sheer chance, of course, and Mr. Mills snatched at the chance to get his message through to you, speaking as I did, into the extension in the drawing-room."

"Bravo, chief inspector! Well played indeed!" came admiringly from Colonel Walsh.

"So that is the explanation of the message that suggested that another man was, or had been, in Mills' flat!" Sewell thought that Mills had been very quick witted. "But why summon Walsh to find her dead?" He decided to refer to Violet as "she," and "her." He gazed speculatively at Pointer. "You thought it might be some one who wanted to be sure that they would be able to search the Ennismore Gardens house undisturbed by Walsh. But if it was Mills who sent the message, he had already gone over the bedroom at five."

"The murderer rarely wants to be the one to find the body," Pointer said, "unless there is some very special necessity for him to take something away, or alter something. Mr. Mills would have to return to his flat in the ordinary way; and he very much wanted, I think, that some one else besides himself should make the discovery that must be made."

"He did his damndest not to go back with Miss Kitty Walsh and me," Arthur said. "I had to insist on his doing so. I thought it some practical joke, you see, and didn't relish taking it alone. Luckily I spoilt that part of his plan."

Sewell looked regretfully at his watch. He had to be off. He had agreed to a very urgent interview in the country at the house of a former client, and he must not be late.

"I shall be back in Town to-morrow," he said in undisguised hope of indulgence. "Of course, I'm now out of all this professionally; but I'm all in, as far as being a most tremendously interested onlooker is concerned."

The telephone bell rang. The call was for Pointer. Mills requested an immediate interview with the chief inspector.

"There!" Sewell paused for a moment to exclaim. "Confession! The whereabouts of the two necklaces! And I on my way to Devizes! Hard luck!" With which successively-more-regret- ful ejaculations he had, perforce, to hurry off.

CHAPTER SEVENTEEN: ARTHUR GETS A HARD KNOCK

"Do you think it is a confession that's coming?" Colonel Walsh asked.

"Or more lies?" came bitterly from Arthur.

"Quite possibly," Pointer said tranquilly, "he has learned that we have become aware of a convenient bungalow at Folkestone. It is the property of ' Mrs. Finch's ' present husband, Mr. Gray; but is used quite as possessively, in his frequent absences on his own affairs, by either his wife or her business partner, Mr. Mills. And the knowledge of our discovery of this fact may have decided the latter to volunteer some statement about it."

"Bungalow at Folkestone?" Arthur and his father were alike seized with the possible importance of this news.

"Yes. Bought, as said, in the name of Mr. Gray, but paid for by Mrs. Finch. I imagine that Mr. Mills, knowing or correctly surmising that the Folkestone police are always friendly to me, shrewdly anticipates my intention to run down there to-morrow and be privately shown over Seaview, as the bungalow is called, while none of its three users is staying in it. This message at any rate suggests that we may find the visit worth while."

"You think he may have cached the pearls there, Chief Inspector?" Colonel Walsh asked with an excitement almost as irrepressible as was his eagerly listening son's look of eager interest.

"Well, sir, don't you think it would suggest itself to you as an exceptionally secure hiding-place if you had such booty to stow away safe from police suspicion?" Pointer replied. "Belongs to a man so far uninvolved in the case; and heretofore not even discovered to be his. Mr. Mills either has or can easily get a duplicate key to it. He may have his own secret cache there, unguessed by either Mr. Gray or Mrs. Finch herself; most conveniently accessible for a sudden flight abroad, if need be. At all events I think this so possible that I should be very glad if Mr. Walsh, at least," Pointer said cheerfully, "would run down there with me to-morrow morning, to identify and claim the pearls if we find them."

Arthur no less cheerfully replied that he would most willingly be at Scotland Yard's service for such a promising possibility, and Pointer got into his car, saying that the exact time at which he would call for Mr. Walsh would be arranged over the phone, with mutual discreetness, after he had heard what Mr. Mills, on being formally cautioned of its risk, had to say to him.

That gentleman was looking far from jaunty, or even well, when he was brought into the chief inspector's official room. As all that he wanted to say was, however, an attempt to build up an alibi for yesterday after five o'clock, Pointer informed him that it was now practically certain that it had not been Mrs. Walsh who had acted and spoken through the bedroom door in that character, at Ennismore Gardens. And when to this he added the discovery of Mills's still-binding marriage to Violet Finch, and of his, Pointer's, conviction that it was Mills who had sent the mysterious telephone message to Arthur Walsh, his hearer seemed like a man who had been dealt a terrible blow over the heart. After a long silence he finally begged for a few more minutes to think out his wisest course. Pointer gave him ten, while he busied himself with official documents in his bureau. Then Mills faced him again, ashen-hued to his very lips also, as he gasped:

"Look here, chief inspector, there's only one man who possibly can save me yet! And that's you! I solemnly swear to you that I didn't kill poor Vi. I know nothing about—"

Pointer stopped him. "Mr. Mills, truth may save you. But be very sure that lies, however clever, will not."

On that, Mills sat with his head buried in his hands for a full five minutes. Then he lifted it to say hoarsely: "I don't suppose, really, that anything I can say will be of any use, now! I've been a damned fool. And it's the fools who get caught in this world. But I'll tell you everything, truthfully.

"First about my marriage. It stands for absolutely nothing in my wife's murder. Nothing whatever! She and I had a sort of mad pash on each other. The clubs were bringing in the shekels faster than even she and I could spend them, and we weren't bad in that line! Mrs. Finch—I'll leave her out, but she's a bloody dangerous woman, chief inspector. Neither Vi nor I wanted her down on us so we got married on the quiet. Then, within a month, came the slump in the Owls. Slump in our funds. And we got on each other's nerves at once.

"Violet was as much a bully as her mother, I can tell you; without the old woman's brains or guts. It came to this—that I loathed her and she me. So we agreed to call the marriage off, and parted. No tears, I can assure you, on either side. I was lucky to be quit of her so easily, I thought. There is an American woman I'm keen on marrying. She's my type. We were born for each other. She going to—" he gulped, and suddenly stared, his eyes glassy as he stammered: "I suppose—you think— that's a motive!" He could hardly get his lips to say the words. Panic shook him for a second. "God! It's not! It's not!" His teeth began to chatter. Pointer sat silent; and Mills presently resumed: "Mrs. Finch will try to make you think it was! Mrs. Finch has been writing sheaves to me about 'the pearls.' The woman actually swears that I've got them! She's out for my blood, chief inspector."

"Suppose you tell me about what really happened, Mr. Mills," Pointer said quietly. "What really happened, though," he emphasised meaningly.

"Nothing happened!" came violently from Mills. "Nothing! I came back to town earlier than I expected yesterday and—"

"Oh, no, no!" Pointer interrupted. "Begin with the copied pearls . . . In Paris . . . Monsieur Delaroche . . ."

Mills gulped down half the water in a tumbler standing beside him before continuing: "Vi was in desperate money straits when she got engaged to Walsh. But his solicitor advised him to insert a clause in the settlements which stipulated that he wouldn't pay a penny of any debts incurred by her before the marriage. As I say, she desperately needed money, and those splendid pearls given to her before the wedding as his wedding gift seemed a heaven-sent opportunity, if she could get them imitated. For she believed that she could sell them separately for a good deal more, each, than Walsh had paid, as she knew, for the two together.

"She consulted me, secretly, as to where she could get them expertly copied. I told her of Delaroche, because I knew that Mrs. Yerkes had some fine pearls marvellously imitated by him for herself. And like a fool, I offered to take them with me, when I had to go to Paris presently on business, and bring the copies back. I had to give her a very stiff receipt, though, and plonk down all my available cash before she made up her mind to let me take them. But she promised to let me have the selling of them afterwards on a ten per cent, commission. To tell the truth, I rather thought Mrs. Yerkes would like to buy them; and of course Vi would have to have perfect copies to take their place as Walsh's wedding gift.

"I got the copies all right, and handed them to Vi the week before the wedding. Mrs. Yerkes, though, did not buy the originals. She had had to go back to Santa Barbara because of her sister's illness. Her sister's dying. Means still more money for Mrs. Yerkes, eventually; and thank heaven it keeps her away from England just now.

"Then came Vi's marriage to Walsh. Invalid, of course; but that was our secret; and I swear that no one drank the bride's health more heartily than I did. I honestly wished her joy! My God! . . . Then yesterday I was out of town with Mrs. Finch; knee-deep in our own money troubles. She decided to cut short the interview we were having with some creditors before lunch. And I, on my part, too, had received a letter that morning, typed and signed ' Elwes Morris.' It peremptorily asked me to come and see him at the Cumberland Hotel, ' on a matter connected with some imitation pearls.'

"I knew at once that Violet had been up to something. And I knew also that it would be no earthly use to ask her about it; for Vi is—was, poor girl!—a champion liar. I was determined to find out for myself what her game was. She had put off letting me sell the pearls on commission, but, as Mrs. Yerkes was still away, that did not matter. You've got to have a long spoon, chief inspector, when supping with the devil! I did exactly as the 'Elwes Morris' letter instructed. Went to the said hotel, getting there by a quarter to four, going straight to Room 3005, and waiting there.

"It was unlocked. The letter said that this Mr. Morris might be detained for half an hour 'about the beads' before seeing me. And as I found, as he wrote that I would, plenty of good cigars out on the table and a bottle of first-class Amontillado, a favourite wine of mine, I waited till four-thirty. Then the telephone rang. Some one went on, before I could speak, to say that he 'would be detained for the rest of the afternoon and evening, but would write again.'

"I was furious, of course, but the speaker, who spoke in a sort of Welsh sing-song, rang off. I went to my flat. Got there by four-thirty—" Mills paused for another gulp of water. "Let myself in —and found poor Vi there!—as you saw her. And all around her body, on the floor, were torn-up scraps of my own writing! Some old letter of mine that I suppose she had found in her handbag, torn up, and flung into an empty paper-basket; then, I imagine, in the tragic scene between Vi and some one else, she must have kicked over the basket, scattering the torn scraps.

"I know now that I ought to have just picked them all up and slipped away. But my brain was stunned. I could only think stupidly of replacing the bits of my handwriting with blank bits. So I hurriedly tore up a paper wrapper—as you saw— and scattered its scraps instead. Then I nerved myself to get her keys and rushed out. I let myself into the house in Ennismore Gardens, my one impulse being to get my own and her marriage certificate before her things would be searched by the police. I didn't believe she had destroyed it, for I knew that she always kept everything of that sort, all her papers, foolishly. I had never written her any love letters; but she had that certificate, I was certain, and I must get it. I knew the old cabin trunk where she would be almost sure to keep it. Got it, and was just throwing her keys into a drawer when a tap came on the door of the room! The blasted parlourmaid wanted to know 'would Mrs. Walsh like any tea?'" Mills gave a honk of hysterical laughter. "A neat whisky was what I badly needed, but I remembered Vi's habit when she was in her bedroom and didn't want to have to hear anything bothersome. So, like her, I turned the tap on, and let the water splash; and under cover of its sound I answered with a light falsetto, 'No, thanks,' through the closed door.

"Though mind, you, chief inspector"—Mills sat forward in his chair, his voice growing stronger— "I wasn't afraid. I wasn't conscious of danger. I hadn't been, even when I found her murdered in my flat—fool that I was! I only wanted to get hold of that certificate so that Mrs. Yerkes would never learn of my marriage. Really, I couldn't have been quite all there! Incidentally, there'll be found her first wedding-ring behind the freshly-gilded radiator in her room. It was just like Vi to keep it! Possibly she hadn't quite lost the glamour it had for us both, once. It fell out of the envelope and rolled under the pipes. I clawed after it but I had to give it up, and slipped out of the house without meeting any one. But at the other end of the street I saw a woman I knew get out of her car and come waddling along. She couldn't see me; she's as blind as a bat without specs. So I wheeled round, rang the bell—I hadn't the latch-key on me —and asked for 'Mrs. Walsh.'

"I didn't mind doing it, chief inspector. It wasn't nerve; it was just that I was still a bit dazed, I think. But I didn't want that woman to see me walking away from that house. I did have that much instinct of self-preservation in spite of my numbness. I heard ' Mrs. Walsh' was out, as in a dream, and then, still fuzzy but subconsciously acting the part out, I talked about a wedding present and said I would go on to Grosvenor House, to see if she was there. By that time I had the sense to camouflage by really going to Grosvenor House in search of her, and met Walsh. And as I stood talking about china to him, suddenly, like a thunderbolt, I realised what I was in for!

"I couldn't, daren't alter my usual way of life. I must show up fairly soon openly at my flat and I simply couldn't face the sight I knew was there. I was horribly afraid I couldn't act sufficient surprise, or that I would say something the police might fasten on. I wanted to get Walsh to go with me, for his terrible shock would take attention off me. Luckily he went downstairs for a book about our argument on china. I heard the telephone ring below. There was an extension the decorators had left on the mantel. I felt sure Vi had been found and I took down the receiver to listen-in. I heard Walsh say—to me, as it were—' Yes; Walsh speaking. Who is it?'—getting no answer to his question. On that I had a brain-wave, as I thought, and made up a continuation for the first speaker in the message you know. I imitated the voice of a Mr. Silberrad with whom Mrs. Finch and I had just been having a talk at Maidenhead. He has a German accent that you could lean on. I was bent on getting Walsh to go to my flat without me. Then, to my consternation, I found when he came upstairs that Walsh was sure it was a clumsy hoax! I hadn't said the right thing, evidently; or not in the right way. You see, I hadn't had a moment to think out a plausible message. And then Kitty Walsh came in, also asking for Vi. And that saved my scheme. But Walsh insisted on dragging me along to see that he was right about the 'hoax.' The rest you know."

"How about the taking away of the little red and blue tablecloth? Why did you do that, Mr. Mills?" Pointer asked dryly.

Mills was still a moment before he said: "I was feeling very rocky, chief inspector, by the time we reached my flat, and I clutched at even a small table to steady myself. I had pulled my glove off as I came in, for I wanted to act just as usual. To my horror, I saw that left a conspicuous patch of gilding on the little table's cloth. I must have got it on my hand—they were both sweating—when I was hunt- ing for the ring that had jumped behind the freshly-gilt radiator. I had tried desperately to get it back, as you can imagine. And when I saw that damning stain I had, of course, to get the cloth away. There again I hadn't time to think clearly, even if you could call any of those half-crazy impulses 'thinking' at all. I just automatically snatched the cloth off, crammed it up my sleeve, ran down into the kitchen, and—once again like an absolutely demented fool—stuffed the tell-tale thing in among a lot of soiled table-napkins in a dresser drawer."

Mills swore that he had had no intention of preventing the real time of Violet's murder becoming known, either when he had let the parlourmaid think she was alive in her bedroom or when he had faked that telephone message. He insisted that he had acted throughout on the spur of each terrible moment. He declared solemnly that he had no faintest knowledge of what had become of the real pearls, let alone had had any share in any sale of them if they had been sold. That he had no alibi covering the time when the "rajah secretary" was at one or other of the two hotels was his sheer bad luck.

"Then who do you think is the murderer?" Pointer queried.

Mills had risen and was standing facing him. He leaned impressively towards him as he almost whispered: "Mrs. Finch! Vi disliked her and feared her. While her mother disliked and despised Vi. Somehow she's got these pearls. I tell you, chief inspector, that woman would flay any one, any one, alive for such a sum of money, in the present state of her affairs."

Chapter Eighteen: The Pearls are Found

Sewell had received a message when he was half-way to Devizes, putting his interview off for two days. Whereupon he instantly tried unsuccessfully to get Pointer on the phone. Failing him, he phoned to Arthur Walsh, and arranged to dine with him.

Sewell and he had enjoyed what on the whole was a fairly cheerful dinner, all things considered. Arthur talked gratefully about the sympathetic way in which Ann Lovelace was helping him and his father by her tact and kindness, notwithstanding her natural horror at Violet's appalling treachery.

Sewell agreed with him as to the shock that learning of such deliberate and even criminal duplicity must have been to a nature like that of Miss Lovelace.

"I feel as though I had been under an evil spell," Arthur said soberly, "to be so blinded. Not to see . . ." he checked himself. And the two men then discussed the case itself with quite a fair amount of objectivity; Arthur posting Sewell about the bungalow at Shorncliffe Road, Folkestone.

"If the chief inspector fails to find the pearls cached in that bungalow, or its grounds, if it's got any," Arthur said thoughtfully, "I don't see his next step." Nor did Sewell. But he felt quite sure that Pointer did, and was absorbed in silent speculations as to possible alternatives, with scant attention to the other's wandering talk.

And when he had left Walsh he got out his roadster and motored down to Folkestone. He himself was now out of the case; free from all its obligations. Nor was it

Scotland Yard's ground. It belonged to the Folkestone police. Sewell knew that part of the country very well. His first O.T.C. camp had been close to Shorncliffe, and he easily found Seaview among a group of other bungalows.

It was about half-past twelve and a beautiful, clear night. He hid his car and walked round the little house in its sandy garden. A wilful impulse was rising in him, as he made his prowling observations. He had a knife. . . that back window catch looked absolutely rotten . . . It had neither bars nor shutters . . . Any one could push back the catch and get in . . . he might have the immense luck to find those pearls that Pointer was after . . .

Sewell took a half-turn away from that most enticing temptation. Followed irresistibly, however, by a whole-turn back to that window. Next, found the thing accomplished and himself noiselessly inside. He left the window as he had found it, and switched on his torch. He was in the dining-room evidently. It looked the sort of place that he would expect Mr. Gray to have. "Cheap and nasty," Sewell said, wrinkling up his nose at the thickly-loaded varnish glittering on tables and sideboard.

There was a drawing-room opening out of this dining-room, with its own gimcrack chairs and sofa; and a smoking-room on the other side of the hall. A nice room this last. Gray had kept it simple. The drugget was plain; so were the furnishings, even to a big velvet pouffe by the curb. It had a big tallboy with all its drawers locked, he found on trying them, facing the fireplace. There were built-in cupboards, too. Suddenly a click caught his ear. On the instant he stood rigid, his own torch out. Another faint click. He had heard that same sound only a few minutes ago, made by himself. . . . Some one was evidently at work on the hasp of the kitchen window. Who? Was Mills at liberty? Was it the police? Or a house-breaker? But he mustn't wait to know which. He softly opened one of the cupboards and to his delight found it empty, with its one shelf some six feet up from the floor, and quietly slipped into it. If it was only some chance thief he might not stop to search unpromising-looking, because keyless, cupboards. "Kismet!"

Unfortunately the door, which he had softly drawn to after him, shut off all view of the room and he dared not leave it ajar. His luminous watch dial told him that it was now close on one o'clock. He heard movements from the man or woman—but the mode of entry seemed to negative the latter—now only too close to himself. He heard quick steps come into the room and after a second the switching on of the electric light. And a moment later the door of the cupboard next to him was opened. He knew now that it could only be a matter of seconds before he was discovered with consequences abjectly humiliating at the best, and perhaps something much deadlier at the worst. His tense apprehension grew so unbearable as almost to make him plunge out to meet whatever might be the consequence. But just as the cupboard door beside him was firmly closed, a creak came clearly from the kitchen. The second comer heard it too, for after one second's utter stillness, Sewell heard him tiptoeing back across the room, the light was noiselessly switched off, and then came the sound of the door being opened with the utmost caution. He ventured to open his cupboard door very gingerly. He was just in time to see the room door being closed very quietly behind whoever it was that had been in the room with him.

Sewell on the instant was out of his cupboard and into the one that had already been thoroughly searched. He had barely drawn its door close again, when once more the room door opened, this time with confidence, once more the light was switched on, once more the steps came towards the two cupboards. The same steps. Sewell hoped that whoever it was it was not one of those absent-minded people who forget what they did last. He did not want him to search the first cupboard again. He need not have worried. In another second the second cupboard had been opened, looked into, closed, and then the steps went to the middle of the room. After some minutes there

followed sounds which had no meaning whatever to
Sewell's quick ears. In vain he tried to guess their
significance. He grew desperate. At all or any costs to
himself he must see what or who was making those queer
sounds of ripping, followed by soft thuds! Getting his
penknife out of his pocket with the utmost care to make
no slightest sound, he softly pried the tightly shut door
sufficiently open by what he hoped was an imperceptible
space. But in the next instant it was flung open and a
revolver was thrust within an inch of his face. It was
death. And Sewell knew it. He was not afraid. There is no
fear at the very end of all. Fear falls by the way. A
whimsical notion struck him that he had come here to
learn the truth, and that in another minute he would
know the whole truth.

Then everything happened all at once. Or seemed to.
A clear voice shouted warningly: "We are the police!" even
as his ears seemed to split with the sound of a shot. A
flame scorched his forehead. The room was full of figures
fighting, swirling round and round. There was another
report and then the figures fell apart, revolved
themselves into one on the carpet and three others
bending over him, while two others stood by the door.
And a voice said gravely: "Arthur Walsh! I arrest you for
the murder of Violet Finch. And I warn you—" The
warning followed. Sewell was beside Pointer now, though
he never knew how he got there.

Walsh lay very still on the floor, his head in a
widening pool of blood. "I'm done for," his voice came
feebly, "you turned my wrist too far, chief inspector. I'm—
going—fast." His eyes fell on Sewell's horrified ones. They
lingered there. "Quick! Hurry!" came in a throaty croak,
"think of your own last hour, and get the bishop of Lower
Mesopotamia here. He's—at—the Franciscans here —
with Ambrose. It must be a bishop—I want absolution!"
And by these words Sewell knew that the chief inspector
had made no mistake. Incredible though the arrest would
otherwise have been to him. Arthur Walsh! . . . Why,

Arthur had adored Violet surely! He had no need
whatever of money. He could well afford the loss of the
pearls. Yet he had asked for a bishop! . . . and only a
bishop can absolve a murder!

"The Church of St. Francis . . . quite close! . . . Priests'
house next to it!—Get him for me, Sewell, at once! I can't
last for—

Sewell rushed out into the night. Chief Inspector
Pointer bent over Arthur Walsh. A shot had grazed his
head, causing a sense of great shock, but the merest of
scalp wounds. Pointer examined him quickly but
carefully; as far as he could see, the man was uninjured
in any vital or even serious sense. He was almost tempted
to let him think himself dying, but he resisted it. It might
possibly have been debatable had the Yard needed a
confession, but the case against the man who had
deliberately planned and brutally carried out the murder
of Violet Mills, as she secretly was, needed no confession
for its absolute completion.

"You're not seriously wounded at all, Mr. Walsh," the
chief inspector said clearly to him, "Did you understand
my warning about 'evidence,' just now?"

"I'm dying!" came weakly from Arthur, who had never
in his life borne pain with any pluck. "Listen! I can't last
till the bishop gets here, for I'm going fast. I killed Violet.
She deserved it! I didn't know then that she was already
married. I thought I should go mad when you found that
out. Mad . . . I'm half mad . . . I needn't have done it!! I
needn't have got to this—dying here like a dog!"

"I assure you again, Mr. Walsh, that you're not dying
nor anywhere near it—at present," Pointer said with
stern significance. For not here and now was Arthur
Walsh to pass from this life. Pointer's whole soul revolted
at the thought of that butchered girl. Tricked, lured to
her death by this callously sordid travesty of manhood.
Violet Mills had not been by any means all that she
should have been, but she was a saint compared to this
cunning tiger who had killed her for his own ends.

"I know better, chief inspector," Arthur replied. "My legs are already cold."

They were; since a shot-wound in that particular part of the head always produces that effect.

"And the cold is creeping up to my heart. It was the fault of her mother," he panted on. "That Finch woman, and her damned Clubs! She'll never tell you; Mills may; but he's afraid of her. I want it put on record. I want it broadcast. Take this down quickly! instantly!" His nerve was so shattered that Arthur Walsh really looked now like a dying man.

"She blackmailed me, like lots of other victims, as soon as she cleverly found out that I had given my word of honour to my father that I had no other debts than those he had already settled. He is insane about gamesters who play for stakes they can't settle. Give me some brandy! I'm going! I shan't live to tell you the whole story after all!" Panic-stricken with his own certainty, Arthur tremblingly swallowed the water one of the men held to his lips.

Pointer held up a hand. "Mrs. Finch gave you back your I O U's on your wedding day, in that so-called packet of sandwiches, didn't she, Mr. Walsh? I thought so," he said, as Arthur's head made a sign of assent. "You had beforehand determined to get rid of her daughter as soon after the wedding as possible? You bought your supposed wife those valuable pearls as a wedding present, and then inserted the advertisement about them, ostensibly from a rajah's secretary. It was you who, as Mr. Elwes Morris, did actually buy the smaller string before the wedding, and after it, as Mr. Elwes Morris, you arranged to buy the larger string from her in Mr. Mills's flat. Instead of which you murdered her with the steel ornament standing on the mantelshelf, and coolly strewed torn-up scraps of Mr. Mills's writing to suggest him as the murderer."

"And that devil took them away and put blank scraps in their place!" Arthur chokingly ejaculated. "He took me to those gambling dens of his and Mrs. Finch's in the first place. He led me on—and let me down. . . . He got me into that damned harpy's clutches and he ought to hang! He ought to— "

"Sign, please," Pointer said coldly as he put the requested deposition before the babbling man. Arthur scribbled his signature eagerly. The numbness was passing off, and his head was giving him more agonising pain that he could endure without low moans. That it would presently pass, and leave him very much his usual physical self, he was much too hysterical to realise, let alone believe, as he persisted: "Ambrose knew. That's why I went to confession to him, to stop his mouth"

At this moment Sewell came back, bringing Ambrose Walsh with him.

Sewell gave a cry as he caught sight of the face on the floor, for Arthur's eyes were closed. "I couldn't get the bishop," he said chokingly to Pointer, who for once had no clue to his evident distress. "He left this afternoon. But—"

"He said that you knew all, before he went to confession to you, sir," Pointer said to the priest on that.

A bitter look just flitted across the tight lips of Father Walsh. He was clearly quite aware of the reason why his cousin had chosen him, though Arthur had pretended to Sewell that he had been too late for a word with Ambrose before the latter had withdrawn into a Retreat. But as he knelt beside the seemingly moribund Arthur, he made a sharp ejaculation; for Ambrose Walsh was also a very good doctor and his hands had passed with swift investigation over the head and torso before him. A fresh moan now came from Arthur: "I've confessed, Ambrose; oh! give me what you can! I've confessed."

The priest rose to his feet on this. His eyes were blazing as he faced the chief inspector. "Have you juggled him into thinking himself a dying man?" he demanded sternly. "Have you tricked him by using the most sacred need of the human soul?"

"Not a bit, sir," Pointer said authoritatively on his side also. "I have vainly assured Mr. Walsh that he has got only a scalp wound. But he persists in believing that he is dying."

"I'm dying, Ambrose," his cousin pertinently groaned, reiterating: "Give me what absolution you can!"

For reply Father Walsh gave Arthur a most unpriestly tug, lifting him on to a chair. Then a look of infinite pity swept over the harsh features of Ambrose Walsh, as he said to his cousin:

"Listen to me, Arthur! You're very slightly wounded; a mere scalp wound. Pull yourself together, and play the man for once! I shall leave you for the moment, to get the best legal help for you that can be procured. That done, if I'm permitted to, I'll see you as often as you ask for me."

But Father Walsh only saw Arthur once again. For his cousin steadily refused to see him until the end, when he asked for him. And it was Ambrose who accompanied him prayerfully on Arthur Walsh's last earthly walk.

"Father Walsh knew?" Sewell questioned with incredulity even stronger than his amazement, as Arthur was driven off between two of Pointer's men. Sewell longed to divert his own mind from the shock of Arthur's arrest. "And just now, when you saved me from following Violet, where were you? Have you got the fabled cloak of invisibility, by any chance, chief inspector? I heard the door locked by the man in the room whose revolver he shoved into my face. I can swear that you didn't share my cupboard. Where the devil, then, were you, to play the Yard's deus ex machina so decisively for me as well as for Walsh?"

"You know the tallboy whose drawers you hurriedly tried to open?" Pointer answered gravely as well as succinctly, for the preceding scene and forced departure of Arthur for the gallows, unless some miracle of special pleading could intervene to cheat justice, was as tragically before his mind as overshadowing Sewell's, who now turned sharply to examine the piece of furniture in question on Pointer's significant answer. He exclaimed with fresh incredulity, however, as he saw, from the tallboy's moved-out profile, that it was a complete sham. It had no drawers. It had no back, but had been held firmly to the wall by two air cups. Its hollow interior provided for the perfect concealment of the expectant chief inspector and two of his men, for which purpose it had been expertly prepared at the Yard. Pointer first assuring himself both of the intense activities of the others at a distance and of the fact that Arthur was paying his first visit to the bungalow and had no acquaintance with its furniture, therefore.

As he was due at the Yard, he had the place locked and guarded, and—arranging to meet Sewell later—drove there speedily. The A.C. sent for him almost immediately. Pointer had already handed in his report, setting Mills instantly at liberty. He was told only that facts had come to light which proved his entire innocence of the criminal charges in the case. Arthur's defence exerted itself subsequently to implicate Mills with Mrs. Finch's blackmail, and with the murder of Violet. But the finding of jury and judge quashed the attempt.

On Pointer's entry now, the assistant commissioner laid a slip of paper before him. There had been an accident in Park Lane. An elderly gentleman hurrying forward had been run down by a car and killed outright. From the letters in his pocket the man had been identified as Colonel Walsh.

"I had just spoken to him over the phone," Major Pelham went on, "and asked him to come here to see me as soon as possible. He believed that we had now completed our case against Mills, and I am afraid that he was so engrossed with that idea that he forgot to keep a careful enough look-out when hurrying here."

"What a blessing—for him," Pointer said fervently. Pity for the father's terrible ordeal had weighed on the chief inspector all morning, and Major Pelham fully sympathised with his relief.

Over lunch—to which the A.C. and the chief inspector had been invited by Sewell, his rooms securing privacy and confidential talk without fear of the ubiquitous press broadcasting it prematurely —Sewell metaphorically cornered his revered exemplar in the difficult art of detection, with the query: "Chief inspector, did you suspect Walsh from the first?"

"Practically, yes," was the reply. "Because, on weighing up the probabilities in the case of each more or less suspect individual involved by the circumstances of the fraudulent pearls and the murder of the owner of the originals, Mr. Walsh afforded, to my mind, the most likely criminal."

"But! He seemed to crave to lavish everything on Violet Finch, as we all supposed her, because he adored her with all his heart. How could you tell that all that was an amazing piece of acting? How could you see any motive for it?"

"I did neither, as anything like a conviction, though. All that I did know positively," Pointer protested with his characteristic refusal to play the occult or clairvoyant prodigy, "was that we had a group of associates any one of whom might, so far as opportunity was concerned, have been the murderer if not the thief.

"Just so! Hell? Taking them separately, a priest is rarely if ever a criminal. Apart from religious principle, he is by training if not by nature much too intelligent. Also, the Reverend Mr. Walsh had a good alibi from the garage through which he had to pass to get out of the house in which he was. Next, Colonel Walsh bears the highest character. I had met him and was convinced of its truth. So, although he had no alibi, I put him and his nephew, 'Father Walsh,' at the bottom of the possible suspects."

"That left Gray, Mills and Arthur Walsh," Pelham interrupted, holding up three fingers. "Why not Gray or Mills?"

"Because, sir, I could see no reason why either of them should stage the murder in a flat which one owned and the other lived in. As for Mr. Gray, one would expect a garage proprietor to have selected a bloodless murder, and to have taken the corpse to some place that had no sort of connection with himself in one of his cars."

"Um-hum," agreed Pelham, "There was no attempt at that, certainly."

"Passion might have struck, with sudden brutality," Pointer continued. "But Mills seemed to me, and Gray seemed to Inspector Watts, who interviewed him in Manchester, to be essentially the coldly calculating business- first-last-and-all-the-time emotionally passionless type, rather than one liable to either panic or frenzy."

"And Walsh?" Sewell drew a deep breath. He had been all out in his estimate of Arthur Walsh.

"At any rate she hadn't been killed on his premises, was my first thought. Then there was the knowledge of Mrs. Finch and the tales about her victims, to suggest what the whole investigation steadily strengthened; namely, blackmail. While the underlying motive to get free from a wife he hated, a marriage into which he had been blackmailed, leaped to the mind's eye, as a possibility, from the first sight, especially when I learnt about his disinherited brother Gerald . . . and Colonel Walsh's abhorrence of a lie. And all his income seemed to come from the allowance his father made him, and the salary paid him in his father's office. Let him fall out with his father, and he would be a very poor man. I learned, though later, that when he had sent in his papers and gone into business— his father's business—he had given the latter his word of honour not to gamble any more."

"Now how did you learn that?" Sewell wanted to know.

"His late colonel let it drop, when I managed to meet him and, apparently casually, have a word about Arthur Walsh. It was at the end of a great many other words about quite another case. But to go back; all the preliminary information fitted the idea of the murderer being Walsh himself."

"You know, Pointer," Major Pelham said with a faint smile, "I rather wondered why you seemed to give so little time to making sure whether it was the young woman herself who was heard at five o'clock. It didn't really matter, did it?"

"Not fundamentally, sir. It only concerned Mr. Mills's alibi, but I had to give a lot of time to him, for fear of rousing Walsh's suspicions. Walsh himself, of course, had no alibi whatever from three o'clock on."

"Ah, his devotion to the young wife whom he had married in spite of all his family could say, made any idea of an alibi in his case ridiculous," scoffed Pelham.

"His apparent devotion to his wife!" Sewell murmured in horror.

"Ah, that meant nothing one way or the other! What people say means nothing! But if he was being blackmailed into the marriage, could I find out when any I O U's could have been returned to him? It would be after the wedding, and they seemed to have left practically at once for the air liner. Then I learnt of the wedding present of Mrs. Finch's. An ideal way of returning letters, or , I O U's. He had left the basket behind, I found out, but had taken the packet of so-called sandwiches on with him."

"Yes, but the pearls!" said Sewell. "The pearls which he himself had bought!"

"And which, if he himself had got hold of them, were still in his possession," Pointer countered. "But taking the pearls by themselves, they fitted the idea that Walsh, forced into a marriage by Mrs. Finch, had intended from the first to be free himself as soon as possible. He would have to make sure of a good, ostensible motive beforehand."

"A sort of moral alibi," agreed the assistant commissioner.

"The pearls would make a splendid one," Pointer continued, "they were bought well before the marriage. Violet was to be given them outright on her marriage so that she could leave them to Mrs. Finch. Walsh would know quite well that the elder woman, whom he hated, would never get them from her. Also, he engaged you, Sewell, an amateur who was known to take only defensive cases; never prosecutions. And yet, by calling you in, he drew attention to the pearls."

"He did keep them well to the fore throughout," Sewell at last lighted a cigarette.

"They belonged there. They were in the very heart of the plan. They were frankly my one hope of catching him," Pointer drew out his pipe at a nod from his chief. "The pearls were not insured," Pointer went on, "though he told the Colonel they were, which meant that no inquiries from the company need be feared. The pearls suggested a well-laid plot, especially the advertisement, and the rajah's secretary disguise. The dates fitted. The secretary engaged a room in the first hotel and paid for it for a week just after Walsh had gone to see the pearls. Also, by being the secretary, Walsh lost nothing. Except— possibly—the money he paid for the smaller string.

"Then, too, the hotels at which the pseudo secretary stayed were where Mills and Gray were both known, but where Walsh had never been, a trifling point, but substantiating my idea.

There was a short silence.

"Did he arrange . . ." Sewell checked himself. "He had nothing to do with the imitations, surely?"

"Oh, no, that was an unexpected windfall for him, though I feel quite certain that he knew there would be something of that sort tried on. Oh, yes, he thought over her character closely," Pointer granted, "and that of Mills too. Given their natures, he reasoned correctly that they would be up to something. What, he neither knew nor cared. He had his own major plot all cut and dried. The more complications there were thrown in the better,

Walsh would think. What did rattle him was that inexplicable telephone call. He didn't want to be the one to find the body. Few murderers do. He had expected that that honour would fall to Mills."

"And Miss Walsh thought Ann Lovelace was in the whole affair!" Sewell liked to bracket Kitty with himself.

"She was!" Pointer said unexpectedly. "In the very heart of the crime! But not in the way Walsh thought. As great as his determination not to be disinherited was Arthur Walsh's desire to marry Miss Lovelace. I'll stake all my future pay on that. He was madly in love with her."

"He had been once," Sewell was impressed by the insight of the tall man now smoking a pipe beside him. "But she tried for higher game, especially as in those days there was Gerald, his elder brother and his father's favourite. So all Walsh's fury with her when she came to him about the imitation pearls, and her loan on them, was acting!"

"Quite the contrary! No man sweats over a very dangerous plot, a life and death plot, and likes to see it blown sky-high. Arthur Walsh's shield was to be his devotion to his young wife. He had to marry her to get back the I O U's of his from Mrs. Finch, and be free—to get rid of Violet, and try again for Miss Lovelace. Yet here was Miss Lovelace telling him something which threatened to make that marriage quite impossible. Walsh met it in the only possible way. Refusing to listen. Refusing to reason."

"He's a clever hound," Pelham pronounced.

"He is," Pointer agreed, "and in nothing so much so as in not trying to throw any doubt on its having been Violet whom the maid heard in Ennismore Gardens at five o'clock. Yet he made one very bad slip. He spoke of his wife having stumbled on some one when she went to the flat at four, and having been at once killed."

"Well? Only a trifling slip, I should call it," Pelham thought.

"I should have suspected him from that alone, sir," Pointer said truthfully. "No husband, new to the facts, would have forgotten the hour when his wife was last heard. But a man who knew that the murder took place at four, who had reckoned over and over with that hour in his mind—he would forget!"

"He passed on at once to some other point when I recalled it to him," Sewell had a very good memory.

"He was planting the pearls in that velvet pouffe, wasn't he, when he nearly got me?"

"Yes." Pointer had his pipe well going. "I noticed a book down at Friars Halt, spoke of it, in which there's an account of stolen jewels which were hidden in just that place. I hoped he would take the hint. He did. Or tried to. I don't mind telling you, Sewell, that I could have sworn when you slipped into that room! I purposely hadn't said anything about the bungalow to you."

"Does it belong to Gray?" Sewell asked.

Pointer grinned. "I told you that the Folkestone police are rather by way of being pals of mine just now," was the only answer to that. "I knew that Walsh was feeling like a hen who wants to lay. He had the pearls all ready to dump in the most dangerous place for Mills, and only needed a word from us as to what new place we were going to search. He was far too clever to put them among Mills's effects. That might, or rather would, have looked 'planted.'"

Sewell sat thinking. "You told me almost at once that the two families were all-important in the case," he mused aloud.

"Just so. A father who had disinherited one son, his favourite, because he had lied to him, and a woman who ran night-clubs which were known to be hot-beds of blackmail, a marriage against all reason to that woman's daughter, and the murder of the bride very shortly afterwards."

"And all that love and devotion was only a smoke-screen. I wonder what his real thoughts were, when he went off the deep end, on hearing about her previous marriage?" Sewell was too interested to keep his cigarette alight.

"He wasn't acting then," Pointer said soberly. "First came blind rage. No man likes to think that he need not have murdered. That all the terrible deed, all the awful preparation of mind and affairs beforehand was quite unnecessary, that if he had found out about her marriage to Mills after Mrs. Finch had handed him back his I O U's, he would have been free and not a murderer!"

"But he laughed! His father spoke to me of yells of sheer hysteria."

"When he thought of Mrs. Finch!" Pointer, too, gave a laugh, though but a short one. "He knew how she would feel. She had given back his I O U's for nothing. I told you she struck me as feeling sold when she heard of the real marriage."

"Her daughter not married to the wealthy Arthur after all!" continued Sewell with gusto. "A son-in-law whom, of course, she intended to milk whenever necessary. A son-in-law who was as good as an overdraft at her bank from the first."

"Miss Lovelace was notified by Watts that she would have to give evidence about the pearls. I thought it as well to let her know at once that she mustn't slip out of the country." Pointer saw his chief glance at the clock.

"The duchess will get her away," Pelham said at once. "She'll have the whole Home Office turned inside out if need be. You won't have the pleasure of seeing that young lady in the witness-box in this case, Pointer."

Both Pointer and Sewell were sorry to hear it.

"However, it'll all come out," the A.C. consoled them, "and she'll wish that she had never heard the name of Walsh before the end."

She did most heartily.

As for Kitty, she still thinks that had Ann been put in the witness-box, instead of being sent "on doctor's orders" to South Africa for a year's stay —and had she been cross-examined—she would have been proved to be at the bottom of the puzzle of the pearl necklaces.

It is one of the few points on which she will always differ from her husband—for she is now Mrs. Sewell.

THE END

Murder at Bridge

When an afternoon bridge party attended by some of Hamilton's leading citizens ends with the hostess being murdered in her boudoir, Special Investigator Dundee of the District Attorney's office is called in. But one of the attendees is guilty? There are plenty of suspects: the victim's former lover, her current suitor, the retired judge who is being blackmailed, the victim's maid who had been horribly disfigured accidentally by the murdered woman, or any of the women who's husbands had flirted with the victim. Or was she murdered by an outsider whose motive had nothing to do with the town of Hamilton. Find the answer in . . . **Murder at Bridge**

One Drop of Blood

When Dr. Koenig, head of Mayfield Sanitarium is murdered, the District Attorney's Special Investigator, "Bonnie" Dundee must go undercover to find the killer. Were any of the inmates of the asylum insane enough to have committed the crime? Or, was it one of the staff, motivated by jealousy? And what was is the secret in the murdered man's past. Find the answer in . . . **One Drop of Blood**

AVAILABLE FROM RESURRECTED PRESS!

THE EDWARDIAN DETECTIVES
LITERARY SLEUTHS OF THE EDWARDIAN ERA

The exploits of the great Victorian Detectives, Poe's C. Auguste Dupin, Gaboriau's Lecoq, and most famously, Arthur Conan Doyle's Sherlock Holmes, are well known. But what of those fictional detectives that came after, those of the Edwardian Age? The period between the death of Queen Victoria and the First World War had been called the Golden Age of the detective short story, but how familiar is the modern reader with the sleuths of this era? And such an extraordinary group they were, including in their numbers an unassuming English priest, a blind man, a master of disguises, a lecturer in medical jurisprudence, a noble woman working for Scotland Yard, and a savant so brilliant he was known as "The Thinking Machine."

To introduce readers to these detectives, Resurrected Press has assembled a collection of stories featuring these and other remarkable sleuths in The Edwardian Detectives.

- The Case of Laker, Absconded by Arthur Morrison
- The Fenchurch Street Mystery by Baroness Orczy
- The Crime of the French Café by Nick Carter
- The Man with Nailed Shoes by R Austin Freeman
- The Blue Cross by G. K. Chesterton
- The Case of the Pocket Diary Found in the Snow by Augusta Groner
- The Ninescore Mystery by Baroness Orczy
- The Riddle of the Ninth Finger by Thomas W. Hanshew
- The Knight's Cross Signal Problem by Ernest Bramah

- The Problem of Cell 13 by Jacques Futrelle
- The Conundrum of the Golf Links by Percy James Brebner
- The Silkworms of Florence by Clifford Ashdown
- The Gateway of the Monster by William Hope Hodgson
- The Affair at the Semiramis Hotel by A. E. W. Mason
- The Affair of the Avalanche Bicycle & Tyre Co., LTD by Arthur Morrison

RESURRECTED PRESS CLASSIC MYSTERY CATALOGUE

Journeys into Mystery
Travel and Mystery in a More Elegant Time

The Edwardian Detectives
Literary Sleuths of the Edwardian Era

Gems of Mystery
Lost Jewels from a More Elegant Age

E. C. Bentley
Trent's Last Case: The Woman in Black

Ernest Bramah
Max Carrados Resurrected:
The Detective Stories of Max Carrados

Agatha Christie
The Secret Adversary
The Mysterious Affair at Styles

Octavus Roy Cohen
Midnight

Freeman Wills Croft
The Ponson Case
The Pit Prop Syndicate

J. S. Fletcher
The Herapath Property
The Rayner-Slade Amalgamation
The Chestermarke Instinct
The Paradise Mystery
Dead Men's Money

The Middle of Things
Ravensdene Court
Scarhaven Keep
The Orange-Yellow Diamond
The Middle Temple Murder
The Tallyrand Maxim
The Borough Treasurer
In the Mayor's Parlour
The Saftey Pin

R. Austin Freeman
The Mystery of 31 New Inn from the Dr. Thorndyke
Series
John Thorndyke's Cases from the Dr. Thorndyke
Series
The Red Thumb Mark from The Dr. Thorndyke Series
The Eye of Osiris from The Dr. Thorndyke Series
A Silent Witness from the Dr. John Thorndyke Series
The Cat's Eye from the Dr. John Thorndyke Series
Helen Vardon's Confession: A Dr. John Thorndyke
Story
As a Thief in the Night: A Dr. John Thorndyke Story
Mr. Pottermack's Oversight: A Dr. John Thorndyke
Story
Dr. Thorndyke Intervenes: A Dr. John Thorndyke
Story
The Singing Bone: The Adventures of Dr. Thorndyke
The Stoneware Monkey: A Dr. John Thorndyke Story
The Great Portrait Mystery, and Other Stories: A
Collection of Dr. John Thorndyke and Other Stories
The Penrose Mystery: A Dr. John Thorndyke Story
The Uttermost Farthing: A Savant's Vendetta

Arthur Griffiths
The Passenger From Calais
The Rome Express

Fergus Hume
The Mystery of a Hansom Cab
The Green Mummy
The Silent House
The Secret Passage

Edgar Jepson
The Loudwater Mystery

A. E. W. Mason
At the Villa Rose

A. A. Milne
The Red House Mystery
Baroness Emma Orczy
The Old Man in the Corner

Edgar Allan Poe
The Detective Stories of Edgar Allan Poe

Arthur J. Rees
The Hampstead Mystery
The Shrieking Pit
The Hand In The Dark
The Moon Rock
The Mystery of the Downs

Mary Roberts Rinehart
Sight Unseen and The Confession

Dorothy L. Sayers
Whose Body?

Sir William Magnay
The Hunt Ball Mystery

Mabel and Paul Thorne
The Sheridan Road Mystery

Louis Tracy
The Strange Case of Mortimer Fenley
The Albert Gate Mystery
The Bartlett Mystery
The Postmaster's Daughter
The House of Peril
The Sandling Case: What Would You Have Done?
Charles Edmonds Walk
The Paternoster Ruby

John R. Watson
The Mystery of the Downs
The Hampstead Mystery

Edgar Wallace
The Daffodil Mystery
The Crimson Circle

Carolyn Wells
Vicky Van
The Man Who Fell Through the Earth
In the Onyx Lobby
Raspberry Jam
The Clue
The Room with the Tassels
The Vanishing of Betty Varian
The Mystery Girl
The White Alley
The Curved Blades
Anybody but Anne
The Bride of a Moment
Faulkner's Folly
The Diamond Pin
The Gold Bag
The Mystery of the Sycamore
The Come Backy

Raoul Whitfield
Death in a Bowl

And much more!
Visit ResurrectedPress.com
for our complete catalogue

About Resurrected Press

A division of Intrepid Ink, LLC, Resurrected Press is dedicated to bringing high quality, vintage books back into publication. See our entire catalogue and find out more at www.ResurrectedPress.com.

About Intrepid Ink, LLC

Intrepid Ink, LLC provides full publishing services to authors of fiction and non-fiction books, eBooks and websites. From editing to formatting, from publishing to marketing, Intrepid Ink gets your creative works into the hands of the people who want to read them. Find out more at www.IntrepidInk.com.